Praise for Alan Miller Books

KIRKUS Review for *A Reluctant Madonna*, an Eric Hoffer Awards Finalist—"Miller keeps this second series installment, following *Holding Court (2022)* moving at a brisk pace... there are numerous subplots...(and) feature(s) a solid cast of characters...the main couple's banter is lighthearted fun."

–KIRKUS Reviews

Praise for *A Reluctant Madonna*, an Eric Hoffer Awards Finalist—"This is a highly entertaining book... it has more twists and turns than the Pike's Peak Highway."

–Rob Jung, best selling author of *The Reaper*
and host of Minnesota Mystery Night

Praise for *Holding Court*—"Both suspenseful and thought-provoking, Alan Miller's outstanding debut novel plumbs today's headlines to tell a twisty story filled with desperate characters and a ticking clock."

–David Housewright, Edgar Award-winning author of *Something Wicked*

Praise for *Holding Court*—"...a thrilling political murder mystery centered on that important, but secretive institution, The Supreme Court... told through the eyes of smart and talented characters a reader comes to really like."

–Hon. Paul Anderson, Minnesota Supreme Court Justice for 20 years

Praise for *My Name was Toby*—"This is the book you would want your dog to write, if he could write. Warm-hearted, loving and just the thing to curl up with on a cool evening with your dog's head in your lap."

–Julia Favia, Sociologist

FIRE FIGHT IN SHELTER ROCK

CALUMET EDITIONS

Minneapolis

FIRE FIGHT IN SHELTER ROCK

Alan Miller

CALUMET EDITIONS

Minneapolis

"There are no wrong books.
What's wrong is the fear of them."

–Bernard Malamud, *The Fixer*

Dedicated to all those who cherish the First Amendment, to the librarians, educators, and others who bravely attempt to protect our rights.

To Stephanie and Peter, who have always been there.

And, as always, to Sharon.

Also by Alan Miller

FICTION
Holding Court
A Reluctant Madonna

NON-FICTION
You Can Make a Difference
My Name was Toby

One

"I'm afraid I'm beginning to enjoy these killings."

The man speaking faced another man in soft, well-worn club chairs. The undecorated office had one large window showing a gray sky as evening approached. The room's gray walls showed no signs of imagination except for a cheap Matisse print hanging on one wall. An unoccupied desk squatted beside a bookcase filled with academic texts and folders of various colors.

There was a long silence.

The first man spoke again. "I mean, I don't really enjoy them, but what I meant to say is that I feel no guilt. Taking a life should leave me with some remorse, no?"

The second man spoke slowly, as though measuring his words. "They were all in self-defense, weren't they? There's a difference between trying to save yourself and a wanton killing. It's more like being an accidental murderer, to coin a phrase."

The first man nodded politely but was clearly uncommitted to that line of reasoning.

The second man continued. "I think it's important that we look beyond your conscious feelings. Subconsciously, does killing give you power? Do you feel more in command? We've already dissected your feelings of insecurity and your unhappiness that you're five-eight and not six-eight. Does this Krav Maga stuff endow you with a strength that's been lacking in your life?"

The first man was Mort Ahrens, mid-thirties, bespectacled with thinning hair. He wore a Krav Maga martial arts uniform—a black, long-sleeved polo shirt with a red logo; black, flex-paneled pants; black cross-trainer sneakers. He had come from his office at the *Washington Post* for a session with his shrink before his weekly evening training session. Mort did not fit the stereotype of the typical martial arts enthusiast. He was somewhat pudgy despite two years of dedication to the discipline.

The second man, clinical psychologist Irwin Silverstein, was around sixty with wispy gray hair and an open-necked shirt under a blue blazer. He wore glasses that seemed stuck professorially to his forehead.

"Well," Mort continued, "that's something to think about. The first killing, three years ago… uh, he was trying to run me down in a truck, and I fortunately had the shotgun. Two years ago, Tommy Tang—the one I electrocuted—was trying to strangle me with a garrote in the middle of the night, but somehow, I managed to grab the severed lamp cord… and, you know…"

Silverstein said nothing, in this way encouraging Mort to continue.

"Finally, there was that deputy sheriff in North Dakota who was involved in the land scandal with his wife. He was about to shoot me with his .45 when I ducked and kicked him through a plate glass window. Actually, in that case, it was the window that did it."

Mort paused as if looking for some gesture from Silverstein, which did not come.

"I guess you can say I'm responsible for his wife's death, too, because he shot her when I ducked out of the way. I never touched her, though. Strangely, in each case, I got a lot of favorable notoriety I don't think I really deserved… and certainly didn't want. Bottom line, I'm an investigative reporter, not an assassin. In truth, luck or fate played a big part in each case."

At last, Dr. Silverstein spoke. "That's one of the things we're working on, isn't it? Each one of those incidents led to solving a crime, right? We're also dealing with your second thoughts about each of those incidents. And your lack of self-esteem. You *never* think you deserve credit. Even when you *do*. Why is that?"

"I don't know. Maybe it goes back to my childhood. My mother always said I was never at fault. Blind loyalty no matter what. If I had shown up at the door with someone's bloody head under my arm, she would have said, 'What did he do to you, darling?' I learned that this was a false value system. Maybe my self-esteem issue is a carryover."

"This is something we definitely have to explore further," Silverstein said. "For instance, why did you take up Krav Maga? It's a deadly martial art."

Mort reflexively responded. "But it's intended to be a defensive one, and it certainly has gone a long way to get me in shape. Remember, Irwin, I'm married to Danni, who is an exercise nut. And very tough."

"Unlikely that the Israeli Army and our Special Forces employ Krav Maga as just a defensive tactic. There are many other martial arts like Tai Chi, which is less aggressive and highly recommended for improving health. I never hear anyone recommend Krav Maga for health."

"Something to think about," Mort responded.

Silverstein glanced at the wall clock. "A good place to stop," he said. "You're off now to your lesson?"

"Yep. Work, shrink—nothing personal—then Krav Maga and finally home to Danni and the twins."

* * *

Mort exited the elevator to the parking garage and was about to get into his Subaru when he heard a woman screaming. He turned in the direction of the cry—the back of the parking garage—where he saw a woman struggling with two men. They were about eight cars away from where he had parked.

Mort sprinted toward the assailants.

The middle-aged woman was holding her keys and a shopping bag over her head as one man, taller than the other, grabbed her arm. The shorter man was holding her around the waist as she courageously used her free arm to punch at him. Both attackers were in their late teens, maybe early twenties, in worn jeans and loose-fitting jackets.

"Let her go!" Mort shouted as he ran toward the attackers.

"Fuck off before you get hurt!" the six-foot, solidly built man shouted as he spun toward Mort and crouched into a boxing stance.

Mort never broke stride and surprised the man with a vicious groin kick that doubled him over. Mort watched as the groaning man staggered into his boxing position again, still clutching at his groin.

The second young man abandoned the woman and turned toward Mort, pulling a knife from his jacket—a switchblade. There was an audible click as the blade appeared. Mort stepped back, let the young man advance, swiping the air with his knife. As the man's arm swung past, Mort lunged, firmly grabbed a wrist and bent the arm sharply backward. The man screamed, and the knife clattered to the ground.

The taller man jumped onto Mort's back, but Mort yanked his body forward, bent quickly, almost touching his knees, and threw the man into his partner, who was struggling to get to his knees. The assailant on Mort's back staggered off-balance, hit the railing and toppled over to the floor below.

Mort reverse-kicked the shorter man, who had come up behind him, again scoring on the other man's groin. The attacker groaned and clutched his genitals as Mort advanced, smashing his open hands against both sides of the man's ears, prompting a scream. Mort followed with a vicious thrust into his opponent's Adam's apple. As the man gagged and gasped for air, he fell to the ground in a fetal position.

Mort turned to the woman, who was still paralyzed with fear, and barked, "Call 911 NOW!" He glanced at the man on the ground and ran to the railing. The other assailant lay moaning on the concrete below.

Still alive, Mort thought. *That's good. I don't need another killing to talk about with Silverstein.*

* * *

"He was marvelous," the woman, Janet Tiberski, said to a DC police officer. His squad was parked in the driving lane with lights flashing. The man Mort had throat-punched was now handcuffed and lying on his stomach, still making choking sounds.

"In two seconds, he disposed of both of them," Tiberski explained. "I never saw anything like it."

The officer called to his partner, who was looking over the railing. "What's going on down there, Herb?"

The second officer, taller and younger than his partner, turned and said, "They've got him secured. Lucky to be alive, though. They called for the EMTs. He's a mess."

He walked to his partner and Mort, who were standing with Tiberski. A sign of recognition flashed across Herb's face. "I know you," he said, pointing at Mort. "From your picture in the papers. You're that reporter guy who rescued the kidnapped judge a couple years ago."

Two

"I think you're losing your touch," Danni said to Mort as they sat opposite each other at the kitchen table. Mort was still dressed in his martial arts outfit. Danni, a striking, auburn-toned brunette in her early thirties, was a stunner even without makeup and while wearing sweatpants and a Syracuse Law sweatshirt. She was hunched over the table fingering a cup of tea. Another cup sat in front of Mort.

"What do you mean, 'losing my touch?'"

"Well—both those guys are still alive."

"*Very funny*. You sound like my shrink. It's not like I tried to kill any of the others. Well, maybe the first one—with the shotgun. But he was trying to run me down with a truck."

"I *know* that. But still, you have an uncanny track record. Your headlines all seem to be accompanied by a death, at least since we got married. I will admit I was wrong about one thing."

"You were wrong? *That's* a first. About what?"

"This Jewish Ju Jitsu obviously works for you. I was very skeptical."

"Skeptical? You were damned obnoxious. And you *know* it's Krav Maga. One of the reasons I took it up is because you're such an Amazon with your exercise routines. It was *my* method of self-defense. And you said I needed something other than walking the dog for exercise."

"Which I meant sarcastically."

Their large kitchen featured a center island with a sink and the table where the two sat.

Danni smiled. "Look, I'm glad you're in one piece and those two are locked up. But, once again, you were a fool rushing in where angels would fear to tread. They might have had a gun. I *really* don't want to be a young widow."

Mort reached across the table and took her hand. "Reflex, that's all. Plus, a little bit of self-confidence. Only two of them, so it wasn't really a fair match for *me*!" He puffed out his chest.

Danni pulled her hand away, covered her eyes and shook her head. "Ugh. After all that exercise, I assume you're hungry, macho man?"

"Hungry for you," Mort said, "but I did miss my lesson, and…"

"Well, I ate after you called, knowing how long it takes to wrap these things up," Danni said. "But I saved yours."

Mort smiled. "You're all heart. And tonight's feast was…?"

"Door Dash special. I had an exhausting day at school—working on student final grades, reading voluminous essays, making summer plans, and dealing with myriad student problems. Plus, I didn't feel like cooking after Juanita left. I fed the twins and put them down for the night. I still can't figure how Dak manages to climb from his crib into hers. He's liable to fall on his head."

"A chip off the old block," Mort said, smiling.

"Or *blockhead*, as the case may be. One of these days you're not going to be so fortunate if you keep courting danger. But I'm serious. He could fall and really hurt himself."

"He's obviously learned how to master the trip from his crib to hers. And when he does, they both seem to be very happy. Anyway, they're fast asleep. I checked them on my way in. We could always separate the cribs, but they'll be in beds before you know it."

Mort got up and walked to the counter where the bag from Door Dash was sitting. Famished, he opened the bag.

"Hot damn," he said. "My favorite—a mushy, cold cheeseburger."

"Beggars can't be…" Danni started to say just as he leaned over and kissed the top of her head. "By the way, Romeo, I'm really looking forward to summer, a little traveling with the kids, maybe a few days without them, if we can get the folks, or Lupe, to stay with them and Katie dog. That is, if you can stay out of combat. But your schedule always seems to interfere."

"I blocked out the time," Mort said. "It will take fire and brimstone to interfere."

"Fire and brimstone is an apt way to describe the next crisis your managing editor will drop at our door."

Mort ignored her protest as he pulled her up, leaned down and swept his arm around Danni. He kissed her again and nodded toward another room.

"The hell with the cheeseburger," he said, leading her out of the kitchen.

Three

The following morning, Mort sat with his feet on his *Washington Post* desk in the tradition of the late and storied Ben Bradlee. He was talking to Alison Powers, one of his team, when he heard another woman's voice.

"Steve Ginsberg warned me there would be days like this," the voice said, almost chuckling as a woman entered Mort's office.

Marcie Gold was Mort's new boss and one of the *Post's* four managing editors. A slender woman in her late forties, with curly, copper-red hair, she presented an imposing figure wrapped in a green sheath dress and wearing two-inch heels. She held a copy of the *Post* in her hand as she pointed to an article.

"These situations just seem to find me," Mort said sheepishly as he hauled his feet off the desk.

"Or you find them," Marcie said. "I have a brother who always found stray dogs when we were kids. They seemed to follow him home, the way trouble seems to follow you. So, are you okay?"

"I'm fine."

Marcie walked into the cubicle and sat down in a vacant chair facing Mort. Alison started to get up and leave.

"Don't leave, Alison," Marcie said. "This conversation involves you too."

Alison sat back down.

"This is your first episode under my regime," Marcie said to Mort. "I know that Steve wanted to take you with him to the *Times* after the

Pulitzer your team got for that January 6th series. But you deferred. You could have been a bigger star there. I consider myself lucky."

"Thanks—I think. New York was a challenge, and Steve's offer was a compliment, but Danni has a great teaching position at American Law, and now we have the twins. So, DC is home. Comfortable. You're stuck with me. Besides, her mother and J.J. are nearby."

Danni's mother, Chickie Rosen, CEO of a media conglomerate, was married to J.J. Richter, Senior Associate Justice of the Supreme Court, for whom Danni had once clerked. Chickie and J.J. split their time between an apartment in the famed Watergate and J.J.'s longtime home in Travilah, Maryland, about twenty miles away.

"Well, we've got two new challenges for your investigative unit. I just came from the executive meeting. I'm afraid I'm going to disturb that comfort," Marcie said, "because we've made the decisions, and new assignments will send each of you off again. I had hoped to pair you up for one of them, but this second, latest situation requires you each to go in a different direction."

"North Dakota?" Mort asked with anticipation.

"No, this will take you south. Challenge one is in Mississippi."

"Mississippi? In June? Why not send me to Hades? Never been to Mississippi, never had any desire to be there. Land of Rednecks." Mort took on a Southern accent. "Ah don't reckon them rednecks will take too well to a nice Eastern dude."

Marcie said, "Look, *Dude*, I want you to take on this book banning scandal that's tearing apart that state. It seems to be establishing a pattern that everyone else is following. We've only handled it superficially so far, but it's spreading like a California wildfire all over the country—and it's a real threat to the First Amendment. They've got a crazy new law on top of everything else."

Mort, still affecting the Southern accent, said, "How soon, ma'am?"

"As soon as you can get up to speed. If you get my drift, that's yesterday," Marcie said.

"You know, I almost got divorced because I left Danni on our honeymoon, and now that we've got the twins, plus plans for the summer, she's really going to be pissed."

"Goes with the territory," Marcie said. "This could be really big, Mort. Get on top of it, handle it in your own inimical way, and hopefully it won't interfere with any plans down the road."

Turning to Alison, Marcie said, "And you, young lady, with the blessings of your boss, here, are off to Kansas to find out just why that police chief swooped in and shut down the local newspaper, confiscated their equipment, and tore the place apart in the best tradition of the Nazis in the '30s. Blatant censorship. And completely ignoring the Bill of Rights, warrants, search and seizure procedures, among other things."

She turned back to Mort. "But Mort, promise me one thing."

"What's that?"

"Don't try to take on any rednecks, white necks, or any other color necks. And keep *your* neck out of jeopardy. And try to keep the reputation of the Post intact. Both of you stop into my office in an hour, and I'll share all the particulars."

With that, Marcie pushed herself up from the chair and left.

Alison leaned forward and put her elbows on Mort's desk. "Wow," she said, "I guess they think I'm ready."

"You were ready two years ago."

Alison was in her thirties, an attractive, slim, auburn-haired woman who had shared both of Mort's previous successful assignments. The first adventure had been the rescue of J.J. Richter after he was kidnapped. In the second one, over in the Dakotas, they had disrupted a foreign conspiracy to buy up Native lands. After an inauspicious and somewhat combative initial meeting, she and Mort had become close friends, and she was an integral part of his small, investigative group. He had made certain to make her part of the team when he was selected to head the unit.

"At least if we're heading in different directions," Mort told her, "I won't have to explain to Danni again how I spent a night in your bed."

During the North Dakota assignment, when Alison had been in danger, Mort had innocently fallen asleep on her bed, managing to save her from probable death by electrocuting her attacker. That bed incident had taken a ton of explaining—and a piece of jewelry—to quell Danni's anger. It had also become a tool with which Danni could torture Mort. Case in point—one evening, while in bed, Danni had said to Mort, "The only reason you solved that land swindle case was because Alison was back in DC recovering from having to spend the night with you."

"That's unkind," Mort had said. "I only fell asleep on her bed because I had been traveling all day—three flights from Costa Rica to North Dakota. I was exhausted and fell asleep."

"That's what you usually do," Danni had countered.

"That's also unkind," Mort had replied. "It seems to me you knew where to find me when you were ovulating and trying to get pregnant."

"That's because there were no other available men around."

"So, you had to fly from DC to North Dakota? Highly unlikely."

"What's unlikely," Danni had said, "is that I picked you out of all those offers."

"Luck of the draw," Mort said. "And now, we've got those two beautiful twins."

Mort had never really understood how Dannielle (Danni) Rose—beautiful, brilliant, athletic and sought after—had chosen him as her husband. It was part of his ongoing battle with his insecurity.

Danni leaned over and kissed him. They both laughed and dissolved in each other's arms.

Four

Travilah, Maryland

A Subaru SUV was parked at the end of a long driveway with two infant car seats behind the driver. The end of the driveway led to a well-tended, single-story, white frame house with blue shutters. A barn was situated about thirty yards from the kitchen entrance. The house was now the weekend home of Senior Supreme Court Associate Justice J.J. Richter, one of the most popular jurists in a court whose reputation had been constantly falling for a decade, and his wife, Chickie Rosen. J.J. was a legal giant, a curmudgeon and an avowed progressive.

Until his marriage four years earlier to Chickie, he had frequently arrived at the court twenty-two miles away on his Harley to the fascination and distaste of his peers. Chickie had put an end to that when his clock struck eighty years of age.

J.J. had been widowed for over a decade until his favorite law clerk, Danni, had induced him to attend a New Years' gathering at her mother's apartment in the Watergate, creating an unlikely pairing. They had been married on the following Labor Day shortly after he was rescued from a kidnapping by Mort and J.J.'s close friend, Travis Anderson, Chief of the Montgomery County Police. Mort, the rescuer, was now also the son-in-law.

Mort, Danni, J.J and Chickie all sat in the dining room with the two-year-olds, Dakota and Meggie, who were noisily clamoring for attention from their high chairs. Danni and Mort initially had experienced trouble conceiving a child. When ovulating, Danni arrived by surprise in North Dakota during Mort's last assignment. They had agreed to name their first-born boy Dakota if he happened to be conceived there. Meggie, his twin sister, was the bonus baby, and she was named after J.J.'s deceased wife, Margaret.

Chickie was feeding Dakota, and Danni was feeding Meggie. Both children wore bibs and had messy faces as they ate apple sauce. Dakota wanted to hold the spoon and regularly missed his mouth. Meggie was content to be fed. Watching from behind, with a beaming smile on her face, was Lupe, who had been J.J.'s housekeeper and protector for two decades—truly a member of the family.

Lupe was a towering, solidly built Mexican woman whose nimble hands and cooking skills belied her size, which was now legendary. She was also the aunt of Juanita, the daycare provider for the twins, who was a night student at Howard University where she was working toward a business degree.

While the three women were focused on the twins, J.J. talked privately with Mort. "You've got an assignment in Mississippi," J.J. said. "Are you being punished?"

"The paper wanted some investigation and insight into the book banning frenzy," Mort said. "I drew the short straw."

"No, they went with their best investigative reporter," J.J. said, "and you know it. Shyness doesn't become you. That book banning is a pernicious attack on the First Amendment, among other things, and I can express that opinion because the Supreme Court doesn't have any cases on the horizon yet." J.J. would never discuss anything pending before the court, or even probable in the future, and the family was well aware of his integrity in that regard. "How long do you figure you'll be gone?" J.J. asked.

"I fly into Jackson and meet a local investigative reporter, then head down to Biloxi where they recently passed a bizarre law."

"What other kind do they pass down there?" J.J. joked. "Anti-abortion, anti-IVF, anti-gun safety, anti-everything that would make their lives better. I don't know how they keep electing those regressive bozos."

"Gerrymandering helps," Mort said.

Danni looked up from feeding Meggie and said, "This just better not louse up our summer plans. For once I'd like an uninterrupted vacation."

"And we'll get to spend time with the kids," Chickie said.

Lupe added, "I teach them Spanish."

Danni gave Lupe a look and said, "Between you and Juanita, they'll be fluent in Spanish before they can speak English." A chuckle from J.J. made Danni smile.

"I think I can wrap it up in less than a week," Mort said confidently.

"You better," Danni replied.

* * *

Mort's Delta flight to Jackson was delayed for two hours because of a "mechanical problem." Then, when it was finally cleared for takeoff, possible tornadoes in the Jackson area delayed the flight another ninety minutes. Instead of arriving at noon, it was late afternoon when they touched down at the Medgar Wiley Evers International Airport.

Five

⸺◈⸺

Jackson, Mississippi

Entering the main terminal with carryon in hand and a computer bag slung over his back, Mort looked around, wondering if his contact had waited out the delay. An African American man in his twenties walked over and thrust out a hand. "Mr. Ahrens? An honor to meet you. A Pulitzer… Wow! I can only wish."

Looking embarrassed, Mort answered, "A lot of luck and being in the right place at the wrong time."

"Devin Leo," the young man said, "with the Free Press. We like to think we're the conscience of the community."

Mort's trip had been arranged by Kalie Grisholm, the publisher of the *Free Press*, a progressive daily which had been struggling to fight back against a book-banning movement that had attracted political and institutional backers. Their efforts had resulted in resistance from book banning organizations and unresolved violence at the home of the publisher.

"What's the first item of business?" Leo asked.

"To get me some food," Mort replied. "Being stuck on that plane for hours, plus Delta's dearth of anything worthwhile to eat—I mean purchase—and I'm ready for a decent meal."

"You'll get more than a decent meal at The Iron Horse Grill. The bosses made reservations, so why don't we get you checked in at the Westin and then you can meet them over dinner?"

* * *

The first things Mort noticed in the homey atmosphere of The Iron Horse Grill were a mounted deer head with massive antlers and a small stage that fronted a massive, orange mural with the name of the restaurant prominently embellished on it. Mort sat at a round wooden table with Devin Leo and the paper's publisher, Kalie Grisholm, a sturdily built African American woman in a conservative blue suit. They were joined a minute later by Donna Lublin, the editor and CEO, a White woman whose dark eyes were dramatically framed by large, blue-rimmed glasses fastened to a chain around her neck. Both women appeared to be in their early fifties.

Mort pointed to the deer head and said, "That taxidermist's delight over there looks like a deer to me, not an iron horse. But I'm only a city boy."

The women smiled generously. Grisholm replied, "I think a horse wouldn't be the best advertising for a restaurant, especially when it's in the name, unless you're in France where you might find it on the menu."

"Hadn't thought of that," Mort said, laughing. "So, these book banning folks—how intense are they? Are they for real or just following a script? Guess I have to read up. One of the things on my agenda is getting to Biloxi and checking on that new law that prohibits kids from reading Ebooks and audiobooks that are 'harmful.' And the onus is put on librarians and publishers to decide what's harmful and what isn't."

"Another of our progressive steps back into the last century," Lublin said, sneering. "I'll give you a local example. Right now, as we sit here, there's a trial going on against a local librarian. She could get five years in jail for allowing a sixteen-year-old to check out a copy of The Catcher in the Rye."

Mort looked surprised. "The Salinger classic? I think I read that when I was thirteen or fourteen. Holden Caufield was my hero. Great coming of age book about the superficiality of life."

"Well, you surely don't read it in Mississippi anymore, except on the black market," Lublin said. "They're prosecuting her under one of our new laws, a tricky bit of mind-bending censorship that passes for a law."

"Who complained?" Mort asked.

"It was a setup," Lublin explained. "The kid's mother is one of the local leaders of Families for Freedom—name is a total oxymoron—and frankly, she's not smart enough to pick out these titles on her own. We checked her out. The direction is coming from somewhere else. Probably not Mississippi. There's no one around here creative enough to have thought it up. We're covering the trial, giving it the space it deserves as opposed to the local rag, which is the favorite of our right-wing governor."

"Five years?" Mort said. "Unbelievable."

"Plus a fine of ten thousand dollars," Lublin added. "But they have to get that past a local jury first, and people are a lot savvier than these bigots give them credit for."

"I'm up for attending that trial," Mort said. "I can put Biloxi on hold for a day or two if that works for you folks. That's a hell of a story in itself."

* * *

The circuit court building in Jackson was an imposing, white stone building of seven stories. "How appropriate for Mississippi," Mort wryly noted to Devin, who had accompanied him. "Magnolia Street. Mississippi. I can almost smell the blossoms."

"That's exhaust fumes from the buses," Devin said, grinning.

"As I told your bosses, I'm just a city boy."

Six

They made their way to courtroom B, a large wood-paneled room with the judge's dais raised in the center of the room, flanked by an American flag and a State of Mississippi flag. Off to the side and below the judge's black leather chair was a box for the witness. The court reporter and court clerks sat in an area directly below the judge. The benches for spectators were already filling up when they arrived, and Devin led Mort down to the front bench, empty, apparently reserved for the press.

The defendant, Molly Backus, was a nervous looking woman who Mort guessed was in her thirties. She had arrived with her two attorneys, a man and a woman, and they had already taken their places at the defendant's table. The prosecuting attorney, a stern looking woman in her late forties, Mort surmised, was dressed in a natty, navy-blue suit. She was accompanied by two assistants, both young men.

Devin walked forward and whispered to Molly Backus's attorney, who leaned over and whispered to Molly. Then they all turned around to look at Mort, who smiled, nodded and took out a small notebook.

The jury, eight women and four men, were led to their chairs by a deputy. The forewoman was Black, and there were four other Blacks on the jury. One of them, a man, wore a sports jacket. The others were in short-sleeved shirts. The women were all in dresses that ranged from bland colors to one with flowery pastels.

The bailiff announced, "All rise, all rise, the Circuit Court of Jackson County is now in session, Judge Kathy Jefferson presiding."

The judge, a pleasant looking blond woman of about fifty, entered and took her seat, smiling and offering a "Good morning."

Mort leaned over and whispered to Devin, "Any Black judges on the bench?"

"Not here in Jackson County," Devin replied, "but a few throughout the other counties."

On the opposite side of the room, on another press bench, were several reporters and a female sketch artist. Mort caught them staring at him several times, probably noting that he wasn't a member of the local press corps.

Sitting directly behind the prosecutor's table were a man and woman in their forties. They flanked a nervous teen-ager who stared at his shoes and fidgeted.

"Shall we continue where we left off?" asked the judge.

The young boy was led to the witness chair looking like a deer caught in the headlights. The judge asked, "Roger, do you understand that you are still under oath?"

He nodded.

The judge said, "You'll have to speak up for the record, because the stenographer can't capture a nod."

"Yes ma'am." The boy nodded again. "I know I'm still sworn to tell the truth."

"Good. Well, we finished your direct testimony yesterday when we adjourned, so now it's the opportunity for the other side to question you in what we call cross-examination. Do you understand?"

"Yes, ma'am."

The judge looked at Backus's attorney. "Ms. Diamond, you may proceed."

The woman at the defense table, Irene Diamond, with shoulder-length black hair, strode to the lectern with a legal pad, flipped several pages, then looked up at the witness and smiled pleasantly.

"Good morning, Roger," she said in a soothing voice. "Do you understand that I now have to ask you a few questions? I'll try to be brief."

"Ma'am," the boy said, nodding and shuffling uncomfortably in his seat.

"Now, when you went to the library and asked for that book, that *particular* book, you went right to Mrs. Backus, the librarian, is that correct?"

The boy nodded yes.

The judge interrupted. "Roger, you've got to give an audible answer for the stenographer."

"Yes ma'am. I asked her for it."

"And what was the name again?" Irene Diamond asked.

"The Catcher…" The boy paused nervously and took a piece of paper out of his shirt pocket. He looked down and said, "…in the Rye. The Catcher in the Rye."

"And you said you were sixteen, is that right?"

"Yeah."

"That's the same age as Holden Caulfield, the protagonist in the book, isn't it? Is that why you asked for that book?"

The youth blushed, glanced at his parents and then said, "No, ma'am."

"Then why did you ask for that particular book?"

Roger paused and again looked over at his parents.

"You've got to answer the question, son," the judge said.

"My mother, she told me to ask for it. She told me it's a book that's not fit for a young man."

Irene Diamond stared at Roger and asked, "And yet she told you to ask for it. How curious. And do you know why that was?"

Roger looked at his parents again. "She said it's a book for heathens, not fit to be in the library. She said it has fornication… and prostitution… and was about an immoral young man… and had drinking and all."

"And Mrs. Backus, the librarian, got the book and checked it out to you?"

"Yep."

"And then what happened?"

"My mom, who was with me, grabbed the book and threw it back on the counter."

"And did she say anything?"

"She said to the librarian, 'We'll see you in court!' And then we left."

"And the only reason you asked for that particular book was because your mother told you to ask for it?"

Roger looked down with sad, frightened eyes. "Yes, ma'am."

"Is that a book you have discussed in your classes?"

"Oh, no, ma'am."

"Thank you very much, Roger."

Turning to the judge, Diamond said, "Your Honor, I have no further questions for Roger."

The judge told the young man he could step down and leave the witness box.

Irene Diamond looked at the boy's parents and said, "The defense would like to call Lilly Abernathy."

Roger's mother entered the witness box and was sworn in.

Irene walked up to Roger's mother and asked, "Mrs. Abernathy, did you hear your son's testimony, and is it correct?"

Lilly Abernathy, a henna-blond in a green Walmart blouse, bristled at the question. "Absolutely," she stated firmly. "My son is a good boy. He tells the truth."

"And what about that book offends you?"

"It's obscene. It's not fit to be in a public library."

"I have a copy of the book here," Irene Diamond said. She walked over to the defense table where her partner placed a thin, small book in her hand. She returned to the lectern, handed it to the bailiff and asked the judge, "Your Honor, can we have this marked?"

The judge answered, "Without objection, defendant's one."

Irene Diamond said to the judge, "Your Honor, may I approach the witness?"

"Granted."

Irene handed the book to Lilly Abernathy, who took it in her hands as if it were a hot coal. Irene asked, "Can you look at the book and pick out several of the offensive portions that disturb you and then read them aloud to the jury?"

"I don't read that kind of filth."

"So, you haven't read this book?"

"Not on your life."

"Then, if you didn't read it, how do you know it's offensive?"

"Because I'm a member of a group, Families for Freedom—God-fearing and good Christians. They inform us of the filth that's being spread to our kids, the filth that's not fit to read, that warps their minds. And we act to get it removed so it can't pervert our community."

"And how do you get this information?"

"On the Internet, from their newsletters, and we have meetings."

"So, what do you consider good reading?"

"I read my Bible every day. That's good reading enough for me."

"But isn't the Bible full of crimes and killing, selling one's daughter, slavery, kidnapping, cutting off the hands of thieves, fornication, adultery and the like?"

"That's more like the Old Testament," Abernathy said. "Not the version that Catholics use. You're thinking of the King James Version."

Irene Diamond raised up her palms in a gesture of how confused this woman was about the Bible she so proudly read every day. But then she lowered her hands, apparently deciding it was pointless to argue the point.

"You mean the New Testament, right? As I recall, that's the one where Jesus is crucified."

"Our Lord's crucifixion and death are in the Bible, yes—in Mark 15:21 to 41."

"You certainly seem to know the Gospels," Irene Diamond said.

The prosecutor shot out of her chair and said, "Judge, I don't know where this line of questioning is going, but I'm going to have to object as to relevance."

The judge looked at Irene Diamond. "Even given a lot of latitude, Ms. Diamond, what is the relevance?"

"I'll withdraw that question and move on, Your Honor." Irene Diamond turned back to Roger's mother. "Now, Mrs. Abernathy, you were with your son at the library, am I correct?"

"Yes. He already said that."

"And you specifically wanted to challenge this particular book. Is that correct?"

"Yes, it's one of the books on this month's listing."

"And when you saw the book handed to Roger, you threw it back and told the librarian that you'd see her in court, is that also correct?"

"Yes, or words to that effect."

"And here we are, right where you promised we'd be, right?"

The prosecutor again rose to her feet. "Objection to the use of the word promised."

Before the judge had a chance to rule, Irene Diamond said, "Fair enough, I withdraw the word 'promised.' But here we are in court. Now the book was not checked out, you said. But in any event, did Mrs. Backus, the librarian, have any way of knowing whether the book was for you or your son?"

"He asked for it, and she gave it to *him*."

"But you already said he's a good boy. Did Mrs. Backus know, specifically, whether it was for you or for Roger?" Irene Diamond asked.

After a long pause, Abernathy said, "Well, he asked for it."

"With you right beside him, correct? Did anyone say specifically that the book was for Roger?"

"No, not in so many words."

"By the way," Irene Diamond said, "does Roger also have a card to this library?"

Lilly Abernathy squirmed in her seat. "I don't know. I don't think so."

"So, the book would have had to be checked out to you, correct?"

Before she could answer, her husband, Roy, rose angrily from his seat, shaking his fist and shouting, "You're trying to make a fool out of her!"

Mort leaned over to Devin and whispered, "No, she's doing that all by herself."

Devin chuckled.

The judge intervened in a sharp voice, "Sir, sit down! You're out of order! If you try that again, I'll have you removed from the courtroom."

Roger shrunk in his seat.

The judge turned to the jury and said, "The jury will disregard this outburst entirely."

Irene Diamond said, "No further questions. The defense rests, Your Honor."

There were no other witnesses, no rebuttal, and so the judge explained to the jury the crime that Backus was charged with. She stepped them through the rules of evidence and told them about reasonable doubt, explaining that to find Mrs. Backus guilty, her guilt had to be proved *beyond* a reasonable doubt.

The jury was led out of the courtroom. Within thirty minutes, the jury was back, and Judge Jefferson asked, "Have you reached a verdict?"

The forewoman nodded and said, "We have, Your Honor. We find the defendant not guilty."

* * *

In the hall outside the court, Devin introduced Mort to the librarian, Molly Backus, and her attorneys. Mort said he'd like to interview Molly when he returned from Biloxi, and she gladly agreed.

As the Abernathy family walked past with the prosecution team, Roy looked at Molly Backus and Irene Diamond and audibly muttered, "This ain't over."

The prosecutor said, "Roy, shut up!"

Mort decided to take a Delta flight to Biloxi rather than drive since a shuttle ran every two hours. He bade farewell to Devin and thanked him for all his help.

Seven

⚜

Shelter Rock, Kansas

Alison Powers spent her time after the meeting with Marcie Gold familiarizing herself with what had become a national cause célèbre—the events occurring after local police in Shelter Rock swooped down and attempted to shut down or intimidate the publisher of the local newspaper, the *Shelter Rock Clarion*, in a misguided interpretation of the First and Fourth Amendments to the Constitution.

Alison had been a media and communications major at Tulane and had sought a career in journalism despite the urgings of her New Orleans socialite mother and cardiologist father that she seek a "safer" profession. They were concerned that journalists were increasingly becoming targets in confrontations around the world.

She had survived a painful breakup with a longtime boyfriend two years ago. She lived alone in a District of Columbia apartment and had an active social life, but none of her suitors lit the spark that she desired. She had become very self-reliant and had developed a close friendship with Mort and Danni after Danni had the twins. She had been awaiting her break-through assignment and hoped this was it.

She had arrived in Shelter Rock the previous evening, having driven there in a rental car following a flight from DC to Kansas City. It was June and the heat was stifling. She had pre-registered at Shelter Rock's historic Elgin Hotel, a National Heritage site. Shelter Rock, a city located in the Cottonwood River Valley also served as the county seat of Shelter Rock County. It was a community of just 1,900 people in the Great Plains of Kansas.

The *Shelter Rock Clarion* had been a controversial newspaper for years, independent and progressive in a very conservative area of the nation. Despite the small population of its community, the *Clarion* had a subscriber base of over four thousand for its once-weekly issue, employed a part-time staff of six, and covered not only the city, but also all of Shelter Rock County. The word clarion was a reference to the medieval trumpet, and the newspaper's slogan was "Loud and Clear Journalism."

The paper had been purchased a half-century earlier by Margery Robbins, a transplanted easterner whose husband was originally an executive with the railroad that ran through Shelter Rock and eventually morphed into the Santa Fe Railroad. Her husband had left that venture and had gone into manufacturing and established a plant near Shelter Rock that manufactured school supplies.

Margery, bored with her sedentary life, seized the opportunity to purchase the paper and changed the name to the *Clarion*. She created a new masthead and became a prominent if not often controversial voice in the life of the community. She particularly railed against governmental favoritism and corruption, voicing those feelings editorially. While she had critics and detractors, especially because of her liberal bent, she nevertheless was respected by the vast majority of readers.

When she was ninety-eight years old, she finally stepped down and handed the paper over to her son, Eric, who followed her work and philosophical ethic. Margery, however, remained as publisher, maintained a presence with the paper, and frequently contributed articles or editorials to its opinion pages.

* * *

Alison had arranged to meet Margery for breakfast at CB Baked Goods on Main Street at eight-thirty. Not only was CB a favorite breakfast haunt in town, but for Margery, Alison hoped, meeting a reporter from the *Washington Post* would be a strategic choice engendered to get tongues wagging.

At a quarter past nine, Alison impatiently glanced at her watch. *I seem to be plagued by people who show up late*, she was thinking as the door opened and an overweight woman in jeans and a loose sweater despite the heat walked in, spotted Alison and walked over.

"You the young lady from Washington?" she asked.

Alison nodded yes.

"Well, I've got terrible news," the woman said, stifling tears. "Margery is dead."

"Dead?" Alison said, shocked at the news.

"Dead," the woman replied. "Eric asked me to tell you. Passed in her sleep. He knew his mom was meeting you here. He said he'd get to you later, once he makes arrangements and all. Even though she was near a'hunderd, you never know. She sure seemed like her feisty self yesterday."

Alison fished in her purse, threw a five on the table and followed the woman out.

* * *

Alison had learned from the North Dakota experience that a local library could be a great source of material for assignments. It certainly could be useful for an assignment where a newspaper was raided by the authorities for questionable reasons. She found the address for the Shelter Rock City Library, then stopped in a park to seek shade from the heat and called Mort, bringing him up to date.

"Alison," Mort said. "I didn't expect to hear from you this soon. How goes it?"

"Well, as far as Margery Robbins goes, it doesn't. She died last night."

"What? How?"

"I don't have any particulars yet. I don't think most people here in Shelter Rock even know yet. I'll learn more later and let you know. In the meantime, rather than lose the day, I'm heading to the library to do some research on the raid and find out what I can."

"Good thinking," Mort agreed.

The library was just a short walk away. Alison regretted that she hadn't driven her rental Honda with air conditioning to the restaurant and made a mental note to use the car whenever possible.

Arriving at the library, she found it was housed in the former depot for the Santa Fe Railroad. She sought out longtime librarian Janice Marquette, a feisty sixty-year-old who had been librarian for almost thirty years. Wearing a blue smock and colorful sneakers, she greeted Alison by throwing her arms around her and saying, "Now the whole country will know about the charlatans who've been running things around here."

"That's putting a lot of faith in me," Alison replied. "I had hoped to start the story with Mrs. Robbins, but unfortunately, that won't be possible now."

"Why not?"

"Haven't you heard? She apparently died last night."

"Died?" Marquette gasped. "Oh, my God, they killed her. How? When?"

"I don't know the details," Alison said, "only that her son sent a woman to give me the news. I was supposed to meet with her at CB Bakery this morning."

"My God," Marquette said. "They've been trying to get her for years." She choked back tears, but some rolled down her face. She put her hand on Alison's shoulder. "I guarantee you that they killed her. Somehow. I've got to close the library immediately out of respect. She was on the board. I'll put up a sign."

"I hate to be the one bearing such sad tidings," Alison said.

"No—not your fault. We've got much to discuss, but obviously not today. How about tomorrow? Whenever. Sorry, but I've got to get in touch with Eric. The funeral? I suppose you don't know." She was chattering nervously. "You'll have to excuse me, but we'll talk, I promise you that."

With that, Marquette shook Alison's hand and turned back to her office, leaving Alison standing in the aisle.

With her interview literally as dead as Margery, and with time on her hands, Alison decided to use the day to the best advantage, which meant heading to the Shelter Rock County Courthouse. To her surprise, like her hotel, the courthouse was also listed on the National Register of Historic Places. Built on two acres in 1906, with Romanesque styling, the courthouse was a three-story stone building. She entered without the usual safety checks, which she was used to in DC. No magnetometer scanning, no handbag searches. The hallways were empty, and the posted calendar of the day's events—Thursday—was devoid of scheduled hearings or trials. Not even a clerk or a court officer could be found. Alison walked the first floor, peering into the empty courtroom and referring to her guidebook.

The next place of interest appeared to be the Shelter Rock County Museum on East Main Street, which opened at ten o'clock on Thursdays. She arrived there shortly after it opened. The building, which deceptively looked like a church, had originally been the Baptist Tabernacle Church built in 1886 and then was deeded over to the county in 1956. A group of grammar school children had just exited their bus and were entering, so she followed them and their teacher into the building.

The teacher, a six-footer in his forties with a mop of sandy hair, wore jeans and a short-sleeved sports shirt. He seemed to be popular with his students as they clustered around him. He was tanned, muscular and sported a colorful tattoo on one arm. After eyeing her thoroughly, he introduced himself as Atticus Duvall and then asked, "Stranger?"

"Probably stranger than most," she said with a twinkle.

He laughed.

"Just a visitor with unexpected time on her hands," she added.

He invited her to tag along on the tour.

Alison said, "Name is Atticus? I take it your parents were enamored with To Kill a Mockingbird?"

"Hmmm, not just a visitor," Duvall said, "but a literate one. And yes, my mother was a great fan. You an easterner?"

"I'm with the Washington Post," she said. "On assignment to cover a story. But originally from New Orleans by way of Tulane."

"A good Southern girl transplanted. I assume you're here for the story," Duvall said, "the *only* story in Shelter Rock these days. About our local gestapo."

Alison smiled and said, "Your students are looking at us. I don't want to take your attention away from them."

The museum's curator joined the group as they toured the museum, and Alison was clearly surprised at its treasure of historical items—everything from the city's first telephone switchboard to nineteenth century clothing, quilts, early wooden washing machines and a variety of dated childrens' toys. It was far beyond what she expected in a small city in the center of Kansas. Duvall stood next to her as they walked the building, offering tidbits of commentary in addition to the curator's comments. He glanced at her repeatedly with an appraising eye.

"I'm astounded at all this," Alison said to Duvall.

"To coin a phrase," he said, "*this* is the real Kansas, Dorothy. Folks back east have a far different view of us, I'm afraid."

"You must be a *wizard* to discern my thoughts," she said with a playful smile.

He returned the smile.

His students watched them and giggled. One little girl whispered, "Mr. Duvall has a girlfriend."

Alison's cell phone pinged. She excused herself and stepped away. It was not a number she recognized.

"Miss Powers?" the voice said.

"Yes?"

"Eric Robbins here. Look, I'm sorry you arrived at what has turned out to be a dreadful time. Mom passed away in her sleep last night."

"I know. Your messenger got to me at CB's this morning. I'm so sorry. Is there anything I can do?"

"No, but thank you for asking. We do things quickly here, and I've arranged the funeral for tomorrow. She was ninety-eight. No need for an autopsy. She's been heartbroken since that bastard police chief—pardon my French—raided the paper. Seems her heart just gave out. They even raided her home and stayed for hours in addition to commandeering her computer and cell phone. But it's a lot more involved than just that. I don't want you to have come all this way for nothing. Can we meet, say, day after tomorrow?"

"Of course," Alison replied. "And I appreciate your consideration with everything that you must be going through."

"It's what she would have wanted," Eric said. "That's what's most important."

* * *

After following Atticus Duvall on the tour, Alison was not surprised when he asked if she had any dinner plans. She did not, and faced with a long day or two before meeting with Eric Robbins, she readily agreed to meet him for dinner. After all, he wasn't wearing a wedding ring, and he was an attractive and challenging man. He would pick her up in her hotel's lobby at six.

She spent the rest of the day on her laptop, bored and reading a novel she had brought with her... anticipating dinner, both the nourishment and the company.

The hotel's attractive restaurant, Parlour 1886, looked like a remnant of the nineteenth century with a polished and mirrored mahogany bar and eight upholstered barstools. She half-expected, given the small size of the city, that this would be where she and Atticus Duvall would dine.

She was surprised when he led her to a less elegant restaurant on Main Street called Bill & Essie's BBQ. "I saw you looking into the restaurant as we left," he said.

"Surprised that it was virtually empty," she replied.

"Bill & Essie's is really much more customer friendly and has great sauces for their barbeque," Atticus said. "Parlour has suddenly fallen out of favor around here for reasons that you'll learn when you meet Eric. Do you like barbeque?"

"Are you kidding? I'm from New Orleans."

The food and the service were everything Atticus had promised. Over dinner in the crowded restaurant, she learned that he was divorced and uncomfortably teaching in a school where his ex-wife was also on the faculty in a supervisory capacity.

"It was a union destined for failure," Atticus explained. "We were polar opposites. And although the saying is that opposites attract, that attraction can quickly wear off. Especially when you have a free spirt on one hand and a card-carrying evangelical on the other. At least we had no kids, which eases the burden substantially." Atticus lived in a condo, and his ex remained in their house. "She got the elevator, and I got the shaft."

"I take it you're not the evangelical," Alison said.

He laughed.

Alison related some of her background including how a freelance article in *The Atlantic* had led to two other jobs and eventually to the *Washington Post*. As the hour neared eight, the restaurant emptied out and was getting ready to close. The time had passed quickly, and Alison realized that she was thoroughly enjoying Atticus's company.

"So why has the hotel restaurant fallen out of favor?" she asked.

"The food was never that great," he said, "but it's the scandal about the owner that is at the bottom of why you were sent out here to do a story."

"And that is?"

"Better left to your appointment with Eric Robbins. It's all centered around the newspaper, and to Margery to a large degree. Poor soul. This horrific situation killed her."

"The librarian's first reaction was that 'they,' whoever they are, murdered her," Alison said.

"They might just as well have," Atticus said. "And now tomorrow I'll be at her funeral. Hard to fathom. School is already closed for the summer. All of Shelter Rock will be closed."

"Well, I won't meet with Eric Robbins for at least another day," Alison said, "so it's rather presumptive of me… but would you like a date for the funeral?"

Atticus didn't blink an eye. "I'd be delighted," he said, "which is a pretty strange thing to do, you know, confirm a date for a funeral. Especially Margery's."

* * *

Like much of Shelter Rock, St. John's Nepomucene Catholic Church was a throwback to its halcyon days of the late 1800s. It was a central-spired, Gothic brick edifice similar to the European churches of the Middle Ages, the arched spire green with oxidation and rising above a domed roof. The church seated several hundred parishioners on sculpted wooden pews and benches, divided on both sides from its transept façade entrance. The sanctuary had a wide center aisle leading down to the main altar, flanked by matching, smaller altars in white. Colorful stained-glass windows depicted biblical scenes on both sides of the nave, giving it a light and airy atmosphere. Overhead lighting fixtures evenly spaced throughout offered ample illumination.

The following morning, after parking Atticus's car in the nearly filled parking lot, they found seats about halfway down the aisle. The pews were already three-quarters filled. Atticus was wearing a gray suit, white shirt and black tie. Alison wore a blue, long-sleeved dress, which she was glad she had packed at the last minute.

Alison leaned over and whispered to Atticus, "I assume the church's name has some significance, but I'm completely in the dark."

"St. John of Nepomuk, born in the 1300s, was from a small town in what's now the Czech Republic," he responded softly, "which is perhaps why the name was chosen for this small city in Kansas. He was sickly as a child and was cured, which his parents credited to the will of God, so they pledged his life to the Church as a result. He studied canon law and rose within the Church, but ultimately chose the wrong side in a political battle within the Church. Following that he was tortured and then thrown into the river in Prague. About four hundred years later, he was canonized by the pope."

"Wow!" Alison said. "That's a lot more history than I thought my quarter would buy."

Atticus blushed. "I was a religion major in college," he said, "but I'm really a failed Catholic."

"Shake hands with a failed Presbyterian," she responded.

A plump, but attractive woman dressed in black with a veil thrown off her face walked down the aisle. She stopped and stared at them before moving on.

"As you might have guessed," Atticus said, "that was my ex. She's going to go nuts trying to figure out who you are."

Father Edvard Hoffmann presided, resplendent in a Tyrian purple chasuble trimmed in gold with a large white cross embossed down the front. A young forty, he was slender with a shock of red hair. Father Hoffmann recited the Liturgy of the Eucharist as he motioned the mourners to stand.

"May the Lord accept the sacrifice at your hands for the praise and glory of his name, for our good and the good of all his holy church. The Lord be with you."

The congregation responded in unison, "And with your spirit."

"Lift up your hearts," he intoned. Again, the congregation responded. "We lift them up to the Lord."

"Let us give thanks to the Lord our God." Again, the response, "It is right and just."

The organist, hidden from view in the back of the sanctuary, led the assemblage in a rendition of "Holy, Holy, Holy", and the service continued. After the eulogies and closing hymn, "How Great Thou Art", the congregation and mourners filed past the family to offer their condolences.

Eric Robbins, well into his sixties with a stocky build and a shaved head, looked very uncomfortable in his blue blazer, tan slacks and scuffed brown shoes. Next to him was a teary-eyed woman whom Alison assumed was his wife wearing a black dress and black hat. Next to her stood a young man and woman, both in their thirties, whom Atticus whispered were their children.

As Atticus and Alison approached Eric, Atticus looked past him and said to the young man, "Jeremy, your words captured your grandmother's spirit. They were very comforting."

The young man nodded his thanks.

To Eric, Atticus said, "This is Alison Powers of the Washington Post. I think you'll be meeting with her."

Eric's eyes lit up in genuine surprise. "How nice of you to come," he said, grasping her hands as his wife leaned in.

"Not at all," Alison said. "It's a testament to your mother to see a standing room only crowd. It speaks volumes of how the community feels about her."

"A couple of bad eggs were in that crowd," Eric said, "but for the most part they respected her, agreeing or not." His eyes went to Atticus. "This one," he added, "is one of the good guys."

Eight

The *Clarion* normally published on Fridays, but in view of the funeral and the virtual shutdown of the city, Eric, who was now both publisher and editor, moved the date to Saturday. When the latest edition came out, there were numerous photos of Margery Robbins's funeral. The paper also contained an editorial in which Eric accused the police chief, Val Cummings, and others responsible for the raid, of complicity in his mother's death. Alison saved several copies for her stories.

The *Clarion* office was across the street from the county courthouse, and Alison met Eric Robbins there on Sunday morning. The office was in a storefront with a large sign over the entrance. Inside, the large newsroom featured six desks with Eric's executive office in the back. The newsroom was newspaper "tidy," with mounds of newspapers, clippings and other news gathering detritus on the desks, news tickers off to the side, two large TVs, and a small open-faced refrigerator holding bottled water.

Eric Robbins had an open laptop on his weathered desk with two folding chairs and one wooden armchair facing it. He motioned Alison to the armchair. She sat down, placed her laptop on the floor and took out a tape recorder.

"Is this okay?" she asked, indicating the tape recorder.

"Absolutely."

"I really appreciate your meeting with me like this on Sunday after all you've been through this week," Alison said.

"The show must go on. It's what she would have wanted. And I really appreciate you showing up for the services yesterday. So, fire away with your questions."

"Well, I've read a lot of accounts of the raid on your office, but let's start with the history behind this whole fiasco."

"Good idea," Robbins said, sitting back and gazing at the ceiling. "The raid was allegedly about us illegally getting access to drunk driving records—absolutely false, by the way—but it's much deeper than that."

"Drunk driving records?" Alison said. "And that led to the search of your office?"

"As I said, it's much deeper," Robbins said. "And it wasn't a search of our office, it was a pillage. They arrived and trashed the place, took all our computers, our cell phones, and a lot of other personal stuff and records." He paused. "Not that they had any right—legally or constitutionally—to anything. Nada. Nothing. None of it. It was to put us out of business."

Alison sat back in her chair. She had not heard this part of the story before.

"We've lived here all our lives," Eric said. "At least all my life—but we're still outsiders. It's almost incestuous the way they've got the local government locked up. Mom couldn't tolerate it, and those on the inside couldn't tolerate her."

"So, how did all this get started?"

"It started with Kallie Newkirk, the miserable drunk who owns the Elgin, which is a national treasure. Kallie Newkirk, unfortunately, is a national disgrace. We've had trouble with her for years. She's a known souse, and we got an anonymous tip from someone local that she had a drunk driving record from way back. That started this whole mess. She had apparently lied on her original liquor license application—she failed to reveal it—and the license was up for renewal. She was afraid the truth would come out, even though we never used that information against her. But Mom did ask her about it."

"Would that have been enough to deny the license?" Alison said.

"Probably not, if it was years back, but she did lie on the application. We never used it, weren't planning on using it. But Kallie went ballistic—paranoid. Next thing we know, the storm troopers arrived, the whole police force plus reinforcements. Six of them and the chief."

"How was that possible?" Alison asked. "Didn't they need a warrant signed by a judge?"

"This is Shelter Rock," Eric said. "But better than tell you about it, let me show you." He got up and opened a safe behind his desk, extracted a video cassette, and put it into a VCR.

On the screen, with no audio, the front office of the *Clarion* was in view as the front door was thrown open and six uniformed officers burst in followed by Chief Val Cummings, who was waving a paper above his head. The officers started grabbing computers off the desks of the startled employees and any other electronic equipment they could seize. Eric Robbins came out of his office, and the chief held up his hand alerting him to stop.

The officers removed all of the equipment, then walked out with arms full. They reentered the building empty-handed to remove more equipment and records. One of the women started making a call on her cell phone, but one of the officers wrestled it from her hand. When she resisted, he wrenched it away. She screamed in pain and doubled over, clutching one hand with the other.

The other officers then went to each of the women and appeared to demand their cell phones, which were handed over. The officers snatched files from the desks and took them out of the office. The entire episode took less than ten minutes.

"I had security cameras installed about three years ago," Eric said, "although I'll admit I never saw this coming. They didn't realize I had the cameras, and they even had the balls—excuse me, Alison— to demand the tapes when they found out about the cameras. I refused, of course, had copies made and circulated them immediately to all the media outlets I could think of. That's when it literally hit the fan."

"I can't believe what I just saw," Alison said. "This is still America, isn't it?"

"No," Eric Robbins said, "this is Shelter Rock, Kansas. Nazi version."

"But the chief did have a warrant," Alison said. "I assume that was what he was waving around. How did he get it past a judge?"

"The judge and our city attorney, who's also the local prosecutor, are cousins, for starters. Everybody around here is somebody's cousin," Robbins said, "which should explain something. Chief Cummings has been here about two years after being on the police force in Omaha. Was a captain there and gave it up to come to Shelter Rock. We still haven't found out what was behind that move, but you know about the blue wall of silence, so we couldn't get any help from the Omaha cops, which stinks to high heaven."

"I have a friend working in Omaha," Alison said. "Maybe I can help you. In any event, how many officers do you have in a city of less than two thousand?" Alison asked.

"That's another thing," Eric said. "Our whole force is just the chief and four officers, so he used all of them and deputized some of his buddies to complete the mob."

"But they were all in uniform," Alison said.

Eric leaned back in his chair again and made a circular motion over his head with his hands. "Part-timers, with certificates," he said. "Send a few of your buddies to an all-expenses-paid training course, give 'em a uniform and turn 'em loose to violate the Constitution when you need 'em."

"This is really hard to believe," Alison said, "but I just saw it with my own eyes. Apparently, you got everything back. Or am I mistaken?"

"We did, yeah, after they went through it all piece by piece," Eric explained. "But when I went public, these local Nazis started getting denounced all over the country—papers, editorials. And organizations like PEN, and several other groups that protect journalists, they actually sent representatives here. The locals freaked. The city attorney suddenly got religion and withdrew the warrant. The judge disappeared, took a vacation. And it was papers like yours—big city papers—that turned things around within days."

"Turned things around? How so? With apologies?" Alison said.

"No, no, but the turtles all went into their shells," Robbins said.

"Have you started a lawsuit?" Alison asked.

"No, but Estelle Stetson did. She's the woman you saw on the video getting her fingers broken. She sued the police chief practically the next day because it was one of his storm troopers who injured her."

"But you haven't sued in behalf of your mother and the paper?"

"Not yet. Biding our time. The statute of limitations gives us time, and when I sue it has to be against the city, the judge, the prosecutor— the works. They're terrified because a large judgment could break the city. Maybe restore honest government. Better to leave 'em hanging for a bit."

"I've got more than enough for a lead story," Alison said, "but I'm going to contact my boss and try to extend for a few days. We've just scratched the surface. I want to interview your employees, then the police chief, the mayor, the judge, the prosecutor, and do some brushing up on First Amendment protections."

"Good luck with that," Robbins said. "They'll be as tight as clams, except for my people, who are still recovering from the trauma."

* * *

Back at the hotel, Alison called Mort. She related what she had just learned and asked for additional time to pursue the story.

"Not a problem," Mort said. "Take as many days as you need. I'll clear it with Marcie. We can turn this into a series if we have to."

"Thanks," Alison said. "This goes far beyond the newspaper office search we heard about. There's a lot of history, double-dealing and corruption down here. By the way, are you in Mississippi?"

"Biloxi, not Jackson right now. Following a lead."

"How's Biloxi?"

"Eight casinos and the Gulf of Mexico."

Nine

A few minutes later, Alison's cell phone pinged.

"Mort?" she answered, assuming he had something to add to their conversation.

A voice, not Mort's, said, "I can be Mort, if you want me to be, but I'm not."

"Atticus," Alison said, pleasantly surprised. "I thought you were my boss. I just got off the phone with him. He's in Biloxi and didn't sound too impressed with it."

Atticus was on a patio behind his condo basking in the sunshine. There was a circle of comfy chairs surrounding a fire pit, and he had his legs up on the pit, which displayed the charred remains of last night's ashes. The area was open to abut the rear of several condos that shared the fire pit and grills.

"I don't blame him for that," Atticus said. "When you said Mort, I figured that was your significant other."

"There isn't one," Alison said, "but Mort did spend a night in my bed."

"Do I want to hear this story?"

"Actually, he was a life saver. At least he saved mine that night," Alison said.

"He must be quite the man!"

"I'll tell you that story sometime. It was really quite a night. And all perfectly innocent."

"Well, assuming that you've finished interviewing Eric, and guessing that you're not enjoying this beautiful, sunshiny day, I thought I'd call and take a shot."

Alison smiled. She was perched on the edge of her hotel bed and had been trying to fathom the tale of horror that Eric Robbins had related about the politics and prejudices of Shelter Rock.

"I'm at the hotel right now. Mort and I might have more to discuss, but in any event, I have a whole list of people to interview in the next day or so. I just got back here about a half hour ago."

"Are you free for the rest of the day?"

"Free, yes, but I'm not easy."

Atticus laughed. "I can see one thing. You *are* a challenge. Why don't I pick you up in about an hour."

"Dress?"

"This is Shelter Rock. Naked doesn't go over too well."

"Touché. I see that you can meet the challenge. I'm up for it," Alison said.

"I'm in jeans and a polo shirt," Atticus said. "Casual is the word."

"Right and right," Alison said.

* * *

An hour later, Atticus pulled up in front of the Elgin, this time in a white Fiat Spider convertible with the top up. He had driven her to the funeral in a Buick. Alison was waiting outside the hotel wearing a loose blouse and blue slacks. He hopped out of the car, raced around, opened the door, bowed and said, "M'lady."

"If you're trying to make an impression, you're succeeding," Alison replied.

Fifteen minutes later, he parked the Spider at Shelter Rock Municipal Airport. As Alison scanned the area, she could see three large hangars and about a dozen planes—mostly fixed wing smaller models—parked near them. She noticed that most were tied down. Several turf runways led away from the taxiing areas.

Atticus led her to a hangar where a single engine plane was parked with an attendant waiting.

"Hey, Atticus," the attendant said. "She's all fueled up and ready to go." He looked at Alison appreciatively.

"Alison Powers," Atticus said, "meet Johnny Bennett, the best airline mechanic in these parts. Johnny, Alison is with the Washinton Post, out here to cover the story about that raid on the Clarion."

"Come all the way from Washington to cover our local scandal?" Bennett asked.

"It got the attention of the entire nation," she answered. "By the way, are you really the best airline mechanic?"

"Best in the state," Bennett said. "Probably in the Midwest."

"I hope so," Alison said, "since I get the impression we're going for a ride."

"Flight," Atticus corrected.

They approached the plane, and Atticus helped her get in. She felt a gentle warmth when he touched her back.

Five minutes later, with both of them belted in, Atticus explained that the aircraft was a Cessna 182 Skylane, and he was the owner. With the fixed wing plane humming comfortably and Atticus at the controls, the plane pulled onto the runway. Atticus had headphones on, and Alison looked around with curiosity. The Cessna was gleaming white with blue stripes on its side and its aircraft registration numbers displayed prominently on the tail. Alison had noticed the name "Freedom" was stenciled in blue on the nose.

Atticus looked over at Alison. "You're not nervous, are you?"

"I assume you know what you're doing."

"Got my license last Friday," Atticus said, deadpan.

She rolled her eyes before saying, "Obviously, there's a lot more to Atticus Duvall than meets the eye. What else don't I know?"

Atticus didn't answer. Instead, he taxied down the runway, increased speed and took off smoothly. He glanced over at her.

Alison said, "Seems like there are a lot of aircraft back there for a small city like Shelter Rock."

"It's only one of our two small airports. It's the best way to get around when you're out here in the middle of the country... if you can afford it. A disproportionate number of people own small planes. This Cessna is a solid piece of aircraft."

"Something tells me there is more to the story."

"The whole story is that I have always loved flying. After high school I went to the University of North Dakota for aerospace sciences. Although religion was allegedly my major, aerospace sciences was my minor. It was easier to get scholarship money for religion, so that's the story. I had hoped to become a commercial pilot, which was my dream. I also stayed the extra year so I could improve the flying and get a Masters in Ed. After college, it was a stint in the air force. Saw some action and got injured, so I couldn't achieve that dream. So I relied on the fallback—education."

"Why on earth did you choose North Dakota?" Alison asked.

"For the weather," Atticus replied with a broad grin. "No, seriously, it's one of the foremost universities in the world for an aerospace education." He paused. "And in addition, they gave me a great scholarship for religious studies, which answers your question."

"Isn't owning a plane like this very costly?" Alison asked.

"Severance from the service, saved up my pennies and got this baby about three years ago. Used, or I could never have afforded it. It was my divorce present to myself—built right here by Cessna in Wichita. In fact, I named her 'Freedom' to celebrate the divorce."

"A lot better than naming it alimony, I guess."

Atticus laughed again. "No alimony. She makes more than me as an administrator—and I told you she got the house. So, I treated myself."

"We're out for an afternoon stroll in the sky, so to speak?" Alison looked out her window as the Kansas landscape passed below. The sun was very bright as it reflected off the windshield, and Atticus slipped on a pair of aviator sunglasses, handing Alison another pair.

"No, we have a definite destination. By flying, we'll get there in time for a late brunch, and I'll have you back before dark."

They landed minutes later in Emporia, Kansas, and Alison was impressed that her pilot had arranged for a car at Emporia Municipal Airport. They drove into the city to the Union Street Social restaurant on 6th Street where the owner greeted Atticus familiarly. After introductions, he seated them at a corner table, and a waitress arrived with foaming drinks garnished with fruit and orchids.

Atticus raised his glass, Alison raised hers, and they clinked. She licked her lips and said, "Delicious. What do you call it?"

"A melon crush, or something like that. Specialty of the house."

After a filling brunch, they drove back to the airport and within minutes were flying back to Shelter Rock. Alison reached over and squeezed Atticus's arm.

"Are you trying to come on to me?" she asked.

"Doing my best. Interested in coming back to my place? I can whip up a wicked barbecued steak."

"You're moving pretty fast, cowboy. I don't mean to discourage you, but I've got to get ready for a host of interviews tomorrow, and I still have to do some prep. Raincheck?"

"10-4. By the way, some of the guilty will probably be at the city council meeting tomorrow evening. Might be ripe for your pickins."

"Thanks. Good thinking."

When they arrived back at the hotel, Atticus walked her to the entrance and swept her into his arms. He kissed her, and she put her arms around his neck.

"I better let you go," Atticus said. "Don't want to sully your reputation."

"More likely, I'll sully yours," Alison said. "But if I'm going to the city council meeting tomorrow evening, I'll be here at least another day."

"I'm a hell of a cook," Atticus said. "And I've got some great wines."

"Anything else you're great at?"

"To be continued," Atticus said.

Alison walked into the hotel feeling happier than she had been in a long time.

Ten

Biloxi, Mississippi

Mort arrived in Biloxi on Saturday afternoon after a short flight from Jackson. He had arranged to meet with Lawrence Greene, a member of the City Council, once he was checked in at the Beau Rivage Resort & Casino. They were to meet outside the casino at a coffee shop on the beach side. Mort felt that this was a little cloak and daggerish, but since Greene was his contact arranged by the ladies in Jackson, he complied.

The Beau Rivage, like the other casinos andresorts, was an imposing structure facing the Gulf of Mexico, a huge orange edifice with 1,700 rooms built in a semi-circular pattern. His large room was on the fourteenth floor with a great view of the Gulf, and he realized that if he had packed a bathing suit, both the nearby pool from the Hard Rock, or the beach were available for relaxation. On second thought, he didn't expect much relaxation time, and he wasn't much of a swimmer.

The Beau Rivage, like the other casinos and much of the Gulf Coast from Louisiana to Arizona, had been devastated by Hurricane Katrina in 2005 but had been completely and rapidly refurbished, reopening a year later. Amazing what gambling resources could accomplish while the rest of the region struggled for years. In keeping with the secretive instructions of their meeting, Mort put on sunglasses and a Washington Nationals baseball cap pulled low over his forehead.

Lawrence Greene was near seventy, Mort guessed, and he signaled Mort to a table. A waitress immediately appeared, and they ordered coffee. Greene was tall, built solidly and dressed casually in a short-sleeved sports shirt, shorts and flip-flops. His blue eyes sparkled as they shook hands. His first question to Mort was, "Notre Dame graduate by any chance?"

"Sorry to disappoint," Mort said. "Newhouse School at Syracuse."

Greene brightened. "Jimmy Brown—he was the greatest."

"The *late* Jimmy Brown," Mort said. "Way before my time, although he is still idolized at 'Cuse. Why do you ask?"

"I'm very active with the Notre Dame alums," Greene said, "so it may be out of sorts—but it's the first question I ask people. Always looking for brethren," he said with a mischievous smile. "Sorry about the secrecy bit. I'm the rose among the thorns, so to speak, on our council. The only Democrat, an active Notre Dame alum, and I didn't want anyone pointing fingers at me if you started asking questions, which I'm sure is the reason you're here. The ladies in Jackson are straight shooters, and I'm glad they pointed you in my direction. Hopefully, with a national spotlight, things will get better. I am, by the way, most impressed by your credentials. A lot of accomplishments for such a young man."

"Thanks," Mort said. "The paper just won three more Pulitzers, which I had nothing to do with. My days of glory may already be behind me."

"Possibly to be restored by your reporting here," Greene said, "although I'm a little surprised that the Post would be focused on Biloxi."

"It's part of a much larger undertaking into defense of the First Amendment, book banning and censorship," Mort said. "Plus, that new book-banning law that was started right here by your local state representative, Clancy, or Lancy… I think. That's one of the important items in my research."

The waitress returned. Mort realized that he hadn't had lunch and asked for a menu.

"You can get anything from a bagel to a steak," Greene said, and Mort wondered if his Jewish heritage was showing. "But get a shrimp sandwich… fresh caught and right from the Gulf."

Mort handed the menu back and Greene ordered for him, saying to the waitress, "Bring Mr. Ahrens a shrimp po'boy, and I'll have a Modelo."

"Make that two Modelos," Mort said. "Now, getting back to that new ordinance which just became effective, the state legislator who sponsored it says that it's not a book banning bill."

Greene threw back his head and laughed. "Right! And I'm President of the Daughters for Dixie. He says it's not a book banning law because it doesn't criminalize anyone except the people who distribute these books to people under eighteen. It's focused on Ebooks and audiobooks—digital books—which, of course, is what kids read. And the vendor is responsible for making certain that what they sell or distribute to the library is not 'inappropriate.' What the hell does that mean? What's inappropriate to me might not be inappropriate to you. So that creates an impossible burden."

"Probably not a good comparison," Mort said, "because I give the First Amendment wide latitude. Do you think he'd grant me an interview?"

"He'd grant an interview to the devil if he thought it would get him any attention. A complete asshole. Allegedly, his bill, which unfortunately is now law, is aimed at keeping pornographic material out of the hands of kids K through 12. I've got no problem with that, but it's scared the crap out of librarians and their vendors."

"I just attended a trial in Jackson where a librarian was on trial—a criminal trial—for giving Catcher in the Rye to a sixteen-year-old," Mort said.

"Y'see?" Greene bellowed, and then quickly looked around to see if he had drawn attention from any other tables. "Loved that book. What happened?"

"The jury acquitted in thirty minutes," Mort said.

"Right on! You know, with some progressives now in the state legislature here, we've made great progress in some areas like education," Greene said. "Moved from a rank of 48th in the country to 39th. Now I'm not saying 39th is great, but it's a hell of a lot better. And that doofus of a governor just turned down the feds on the child food program. Kids won't get federal help with meals during the summer break. He says it'll expand the welfare state. Asinine! So, kids'll go hungry when they're out of school this summer, which they already are, while he feeds his fat face."

"Well, I can only take on one crusade at a time," Mort said, "so I'll stick to book banning on this trip. I want to check in with some local librarians and then get back to Jackson. Try to see the governor, among others."

"Good luck with that," Greene said sarcastically. "If you're checking out bookstores as well as librarians, make certain that you get to a shop called 'Banned-Aid.' It's a new bookstore downtown. The owner, Molly Perkins, a well-known writer you probably know, is a great gal and has taken a lot of heat from the crazies because she won't take books off her shelves just because some nut finds something offensive in them. She's not even officially open yet, and they've already hauled her before the city council on trumped up violations complaining about some of the book titles and authors she'll carry. But she's not breaking any law, so we didn't get involved... fortunately. But there've been threats. Serious threats. She lives right behind the store, so she's easy to locate."

"I'll make that a definite," Mort said.

With that, Greene got up, shook hands again and said, "I better get out of here before someone figures out who you are. I've got enough trouble trying to hold up the sane side of our city without more complications."

Greene hesitated. "I don't want to leave you with the wrong impression. There are a lot of folks, on both sides of the aisle, who are very concerned about these threats of book banning. They speak to me on the QT, but they're concerned. Not just about book banning and censorship, but about other threats they see to democracy—even down here in Mississippi. So, it's folks like you who can speak out without fear that are so important."

"I appreciate your time and advice."

"One more thing," Greene said. "Let me give you Molly's phone number. She's definitely around over the weekend with the store about to open, and maybe you can get her perspective as well." With that he took out his cell phone, and Mort copied her number onto his.

Greene left before Mort had finished his po'boy and Modelo. The heat was oppressive, but a breeze from the Gulf made it tolerable.

Eleven

Molly Perkins said she'd be happy to meet with Mort the following morning, Sunday. He thought twice about taking a walk in the heat of the late afternoon, so he asked the concierge to call him a cab. Minutes later, a Regency Taxi pulled in front of the hotel. The driver was a young Black man named Josh Brown, and Mort inquired about a trip around the downtown area.

"You want the Executive Tour of Biloxi, which takes about twenty minutes, or do you want the Grand Prix, which takes thirty? We're not exactly the Big Apple."

Mort liked the driver's sarcastic sense of humor. "I'm from DC not the Big Apple."

"You a gambler or an angler? Not much else in Biloxi."

"Journalist—newspaper reporter," Mort said.

"What are you journaling?"

"A series on book banning. One of the people I want to interview is the owner of 'Banned-Aid,' the new bookstore in town."

"You got a Kevlar vest?" Josh asked.

"Is it that bad?"

"These folks're crazier'n hell," Josh said. "They'd ban anything that even hints of sex, or anything progressive. LGTBQ? Forget it. They'd take us back to the Dark Ages!"

"You're my kind of guy," Mort said, as they were driving around. "What's your background?"

Josh replied, "I'm in my last year at the Coastal Research Center of the U here in Biloxi. Studying renewable and non-renewable resources. I drive summers and weekends. Pays for my food. Tell you what. I'll drive you there."

They drove to US 100, hung a left before the Golden Nugget and then moved inland.

"This is still Biloxi?" Mort asked.

"The protected side," Josh said. "Well, sort of. Lot of land, not that many people. Katrina knocked the shit out of everything." He took a left on US 10, and Mort caught a view of the university extension, a series of modern buildings on Popps Ferry Rd. "Tell ya what," Josh said, "I'll be happy to be your driver while you're here. How long do you guess?"

"A day or two at the most," Mort said, "then back to Jackson." They agreed that for two hundred bucks for two days, Josh would be available, then headed back to the Beau Rivage.

Mort spent the balance of the day having dinner at the hotel and then stopped in at the casino for a look, assigning himself a gambling limit of fifty dollars. He had no appetite for gambling. In half an hour, however, his fifty had grown to three hundred and he called it quits.

"Just won big at the blackjack table," he told Danni when he checked with her. "How are you and the kids?"

"Bored, waiting for you and our vacation," she said. "And stay away from the tables. That was beginner's luck."

* * *

Banned-Aid was a low-slung, one-story building that had previously been a hair salon. Molly Perkins, the author of two bestsellers and one of the most prominent Black authors in the nation, was a woman in her fifties with a no-nonsense expression, serious eyebrows scowling over dark eyes, and prominent cheeks liberally bathed in rouge. She was a slender five-footer and had created the retail space with shelves brimming with books categorized by subject, a space for new titles, a reading room, a children's area decorated with paintings of children's favorites, and many display tables that could be moved to accommodate chairs for presentations and lectures.

The outside of the building, painted a soothing blue, was decorated with a large Banned-Aid mural in the form of an elongated bandage with the names of authors, all of whom had books on banned lists, including Ernest Hemingway, Toni Morrison, George Orwell, Vladimir Nabokov, Maya Angelou, and many others. When Mort introduced himself, she greeted him warmly, surprised that the *Washington Post* had come all the way to Biloxi for its proposed feature story. Mort explained that "finding you was a real bonus. I came down because of that new book-banning legislation that is allegedly *not* book-banning legislation. I'm really happy to have found you. Or rather, to have you pointed out by a man who shall remain nameless."

"I can guess that name. Lawrence is one of the good ones," Molly said without hesitation.

"I love the name of your store."

Perkins slapped a hand to her forehead. "Would you believe it? Johnson & Johnson is suing me. They claim I'm infringing on the copyright of their bandages. But my attorney says they'll lose. There are a lot of people stopping by with encouragement as I approach the official grand opening tomorrow evening. I'd be honored to have you as one of the speakers."

"I'm here for my story on the controversial legislation. I'll stick to that, although I'm flattered by the invitation," Mort said. "But I don't want to compromise you or my job."

Perkins showed Mort around, pointing out shelves stocked with books and a section specifically for books banned in various states but also texts of local authors. Molly said there were over seven thousand titles already in the shop. She had a comfortable, two-bedroom apartment in the rear of the building, complete with an office. It was set up so that she had plenty of time for her writing, with several employees handling the front.

She got water from a vending machine, and they sat at one of the tables in the main area of the shop.

"When did you get the idea for the store?" Mort asked. "Didn't you have enough to do with writing, appearances, signings and so on?"

"One of my books, as you may know, is about America's history with the Black community," Molly said. "Strictly historical, innocuous, apolitical—just the facts. Then it got banned in several libraries, one right here in Mississippi, and I said, 'This will not stand.' I decided right then to open a bookstore. I've already had pressure locally. I had already found this location, so the city council jumped on me about non-existent zoning regulations or phony violations. Lawrence stepped up, my attorney got involved, and of course we won. Then came the threats—some on the phone, some on the internet, always from nameless cowards. Even a sign at the entrance—'Biloxi is no place for the Godless.' But a lot of the good folks, and we have many, stepped forward in my defense. People want their freedom whether in literature or their lives."

"Well, I give you a lot of credit," Mort said. "And I admire your courage."

"Courage? I grew up as a Black in Biloxi. But things have changed, and I've lived to see it. I wasn't brave. I just wasn't going to be intimidated by the lunatic fringe."

Mort's intended short visit extended for another hour. He walked through the store again, took photos with his cell phone, and promised to stop in the following evening after his interviews to see the official opening day crowd.

* * *

Mort was still asleep the following morning when his room phone rang. The clock said it was 6:43.

"Mort!" an excited Josh Brown shouted. "You better come. The bookstore blew up last night."

Twelve

Mort dressed and was out of the room in minutes. Josh was waiting downstairs in the taxi, and Mort jumped into the front seat.

"What the hell happened?" Mort said, anxiously.

"All I know is that a report went out about an explosion and fire. I monitor the police channel because it's a good way to pick up business after car crashes and all."

Five minutes later, they were a block away from what had been the bookstore. Police cars, ambulances and fire trucks were outside the building, and the street was blocked off. A young police officer held up his hand as if directing traffic and said, "Stop! You can't go in there."

Mort held up his press pass, never breaking stride as he rapidly walked past the cop. "Press," he said in his best authoritative voice. Josh was with him and echoed, "Press," although he didn't have any press identification. The young officer looked confused and let them pass.

"That was impressive," Josh said, as they fast walked to the scene.

The bookstore was a mass of smoldering rubble. Water from fire hoses made hissing sounds as it hit the remnants of Banned-Aid. Other than the fire and police, there was no one else close to the remains except two EMTs who stood beside their ambulance. Mort went straight to them.

"Where's Molly Perkins?" Mort asked, craning his neck and looking around.

"If you're talking about the owner," a female EMT said, "she's probably buried somewhere in there."

"I was just talking to her a few hours ago," Mort said. "Think it was intentional?"

"Maybe you ought to talk to the fire marshal," the EMT said, turning her head. "That's him over there in the white helmet."

Walking up to the fire marshal dressed in protective gear, Mort said, "Excuse me, but have you located Ms. Perkins?"

"Who are you?" the marshal said abruptly.

"Mort Ahrens. I'm a friend."

"How the hell did you get past the police line? We've got the area blocked off."

"I'm with the Washington Post," Mort said. "I'm here in Biloxi covering a story."

"I don't care if you're with the Saturday Evening Post," the fire marshal barked. "This is a possible crime scene, and you got no business here. Now get the hell back or I'll have you arrested."

"She's been threatened recently," Mort said.

"I told you to get back, and I mean it. This was a propane explosion, it looks like. Those damn tanks go up all the time. Now get." Mort and Josh retreated to a block away, but Mort managed to take out his cell phone and snap a few pictures as they retreated.

"Well," Josh said, "that went well."

They watched for about an hour as rescue efforts continued. A black vehicle, similar to an SUV but larger, appeared on the scene and drove to the building's ruins.

"That's the medical examiner," Josh said.

"Means only one thing," Mort said angrily. "Molly didn't make it. The bastards blew up the store and killed her. I can't believe it! This is way out of control. Let's get out of here."

Mort was alarmed to suddenly find himself again covering a possible murder case. He called Hailee Sibley, the librarian he wanted to interview. One or two Monday interviews would wrap up his time in Biloxi, give him some additional time in Jackson, and then he could hop on a plane and be back in DC by midweek. He'd write his story, or two stories on consecutive days—now including the disaster at the bookstore—and then spend time with Danni and the twins. If they were lucky, they would get away for that oft-interrupted vacation.

Hailee Sibley had already heard the news. "I got a phone call from a friend. I can't believe she's gone," Sibley said. "She was a great person, in addition to being a fine writer. And all that effort to open the bookstore! What a tragedy."

"A crime, I'm pretty sure. They murdered her. I think she was targeted."

"The reports that I'm hearing on the early morning news," Sibley said, "are that it was a propane leak in the tank she had at the back of the store. It was near the apartment she built for herself. Probably wasn't installed properly. Blew up in the middle of the night. Maybe she smelled gas or something, switched on a light and triggered the explosion."

"And maybe," Mort said sarcastically, "the Gulf of Mexico will part like the Nile did in the Old Testament."

"Do you *really* think that someone killed her?" Sibley asked. "Would they go that far? We're only talking about a bookstore and a few books. Who would take it to that extreme? I just can't get my head around that. The fire marshal—I just saw him on television—he said it was propane. Definitely. End of investigation, he said."

"Well, I met him earlier. Not a pleasant meeting, but in any event, what are the chances I could spend some time with you today and talk about the book banning situation here as you experienced it? I've got to write the story about this disaster and send it off. What about this afternoon?"

They agreed that Sibley would meet with Mort late in the afternoon at the Biloxi Public Library. She had relatives visiting. She'd meet him where there would be no interruptions, and they could talk. Mort told Josh of his plans and was driven back to the Beau Rivage. Josh said he'd pick Mort up in the afternoon and drive him to the library.

"This is a lot more than you bargained for," Mort said. "I think we have to renegotiate your stipend."

"We're good," Josh said. "This is quite an education for me."

* * *

Once he was back in his room, Mort powered up his laptop to do a little research before writing his story. Sitting in front of the window looking out at the Gulf of Mexico, he thought about the recent events for a few minutes, then started writing. His suspicions were not important to the story. He had to report the facts as they had been described and leave his suspicions for later.

When his cell phone rang, the screen told him it was Lawrence Greene, the city councilman.

"Mr. Greene," Mort said.

"I have no doubt you know of today's tragedy," Greene said.

"I was at the scene earlier. Just getting ready to file a story," Mort said, "and I'm reporting it as your fire marshal concluded—that it's a propane leak. But frankly, I think that's bullshit. I think she was killed. According to your fire marshal—a totally unlikeable human being, by the way—the case is closed. Without a shred of emotion, he called Molly's death a terrible tragedy."

"Cletus McNair Junior. I served with his father in 'Nam," Greene said, "but that apple fell far from the tree. His father was a prince. We were in demolitions. Saved my life several times."

"Demolitions?" Mort said. A thunderbolt of deductive reasoning struck him. "Can you meet with me for a few minutes—same place as yesterday? It'll be quick, but I need to pick your brain."

"Sure. But I'm not sure there's much to pick."

Thirteen

Mort didn't bother with the disguise he used yesterday. He was in his shirt sleeves, sitting at the table and wiping his glasses and sweaty brow when Greene arrived. Greene had been working in his garden and was in shorts and a dirt-stained Notre Dame T-shirt.

Mort got right to the point. "You said you were in demolitions. That means explosives? Roadside bombs?"

"The Full Monty," Greene said. "That's how Clete saved my life. But Junior isn't a carbon copy of his dad, who died from cancer about four years ago."

"I never even got Junior's name, he was so abrupt. Threatened to arrest me," Mort said. "In any event, he was certain that Molly's death was a propane explosion. Strange how he could be that certain before doing an investigation. What can you tell me about propane? Does it leave any residuals?"

"We didn't do much with propane, except during training," Greene said, "We worked with C4, TNT and other explosives. But I know that propane is manufactured with an odorant called ethyl mercaptan to make it easily detectable to the nose if there's a leak. Has a foul odor. It's feasible that she smelled something, switched on the light, and everything blew sky high."

"But she was a very smart lady. Smart enough to know the danger signs… smart enough to get out and call for help instead of blowing herself up. You say you worked with C4?"

"Putty in my hands, literally. That stuff is like Play-Doh… until you arm it."

"Odor?"

"Smells like tar or pitch, sort of a petroleum or coal-like smell. A lot of other explosives have an almond-like smell. Not TNT, though. Why? You got any clues?"

"Curious, that's all."

"I know you're an investigative reporter," Greene said, "but be careful you don't bite off more than you can chew. Or your own nose. These are some nasty folks down here."

"I'll keep that in mind," Mort said, "but I'll be out of your hair tomorrow. Just need a couple more interviews."

* * *

Mort met Hailee Sibley late in the afternoon at the library, and she showed him a list she had been given of books the library board had directed her to remove from the shelves. The titles included books like *Tom Sawyer* by Mark Twain, John Steinbeck's *The Grapes of Wrath*, *Beloved* by Toni Morrison, *Charlotte's Web* by E.B. White, even a classic by the Scottish novelist and playwright J.M. Barrie called *Peter Pan*.

She had protested removing the books in the closed-door meeting and had been threatened with losing her job. The "inappropriate" books had been removed—forty-four of them—and now rested on shelves in the storage room. The books included classics, major prize winners and almost anything that could be taken to have a sexual connotation. Books about gay life or LGBTQ issues were removed without any discussion. The directive from the Harrison County Library Board was clear and unanimous.

"People didn't even have an opportunity to protest, be present or be heard," Sibley said. "I was told it was an 'unofficial' meeting so it circumvented the statute in the Mississippi Code that requires meetings to be public, open and on notice."

"And you couldn't go public?" Mort asked.

"I've got twenty-three years into my career and two kids in college," Sibley said. "I was warned in no uncertain terms that if I went public it would be my job. But it's getting worse. I just can't take it anymore. It's got to stop, especially now. It's criminal, so let the chips fall where they may."

"I'll try to keep your name out of it," Mort said sympathetically.

He left a few minutes later with a copy of the list of banned books.

* * *

When Josh picked him up outside the library on Howard Street, it was almost dinner time, and Mort had been thinking about checking out the site of the former bookstore after dark when the location was deserted. He asked Josh to join him for dinner. They had a casual meal at McElroy's Harbor House on Beach Boulevard, a recommendation by Josh that offered a wide selection of fish and seafood. By the time they finished eating, night had fallen, and Mort asked Josh to drop him off near the explosion site.

"What you got in mind?" Josh asked.

"I just want to nose around and satisfy myself that it was a propane explosion," Mort said.

"You know what they say about curiosity. You got expertise?" Josh said.

"A nose for news. Or smells. Just a quick look in the dark is all I need. Just drop me and take off. I'll find my way back. I practically feel like a native here."

When they got near the site, the area was completely dark. Police tape around the building warned them to stay out of the area, but there were no guards.

"You gonna cross the tape line?" Josh asked.

"Just a couple minutes for a fast look-see."

"I'll wait," Josh said.

"No, you get out of here. I've got my press credentials in case someone comes along."

Josh dropped Mort on the street side of the ruins. The sidewalk was still blocked by police tape. A fire truck was parked nearby, but no one was in the area.

Mort scooted under the tape and started looking around, examining the wreckage as best he could in the darkness. There were pages of books fluttering in a slight breeze, other debris on the ground. He walked the length of the building, then around to the back, finally ending up in front where the entrance had been.

It was hard to imagine that only a day before he had spoken with Molly Perkins and shared her excitement about the opening. And now that dream was gone. And worse, so was Molly.

Mort sniffed the air and detected what he thought was the scent of petroleum or something similar. He remembered what Lawrence Greene had said about propane—it had a distinct foul odor, like rotten cabbage or the odor of a skunk. His interest was heightened by what Greene said about C4 and its tarlike, almost petroleum-based smell. C4 didn't get there by accident, which would lead to a far more sinister plot that would be inconsistent with the fire marshal's hasty conclusion. This was definitely *not* a foul odor—not the odor of propane.

He spotted the cover of a book and picked it up, then studied it under the illumination of the flashlight on his phone. It was the charred cover of a book called *Gender Queer*.

And then Mort's world went black.

Fourteen

Mort's eyes fluttered, and he heard faint voices that sounded almost like whispering. He wondered if he was dead and hearing commentary from angels—or demons. He struggled to open his eyes, but the light seemed too brilliant, blinding. Is this what heaven was like? Or hell?

He forced his eyes open wider, squinting. The face hovering over him was a beautiful, female face with soft, sensuous lips showing the hint of a smile. Her long, soft hair, brown with just a touch of auburn, almost formed a halo around her face, accenting intense blue eyes. She seemed so close she could only be an angel. But this angel was one he had seen before, when he was alive. He knew her. He tried to reach out.

"Danni?" he said weakly. "Danni, is that you?" He felt his hand being squeezed. But Danni was not one to hold hands, so who was it? Was he delirious and not dead?

"Whe... where am I?"

The voice that responded was definitely Danni's. "Can't I trust you to go anywhere without getting into trouble?"

"Where am I? How did you get here?"

"You're in Biloxi, Mississippi. At Merit Health Hospital. You've been out for two days. You've got a serious concussion. But what did you expect from nosing around someplace where you had no business to be and was roped off by police tape?"

A young, Black nurse leaned over and said, "Mr. Ahrens... we're so happy you're awake. Does anything hurt"

"My pride."

"I've got to take your pulse, your oxygen, and do a few tests," the nurse said. "Then you need to rest."

"Apparently I've been resting for two days," Mort said as he tried to push himself up, only to collapse back on the bed. "What the hell happened?"

"I'm not going anywhere," Danni said, "so follow orders and we'll bring you up to date."

* * *

Mort closed his eyes and was out cold for the next four hours. When he awoke, feeling much better—except for a wicked headache—Danni was at his side and explained.

"You were where you weren't supposed to be, of course," Danni said. "Trespassing. And you were struck in the head by a metal baton."

"A metal baton? Where did that come from?"

"From the hand of the fire marshal, that's who," Danni said.

"The fire marshal—what's his name?—Cletus something or other. He did this to me?"

"He not only did it to you, but apparently was ready to do much worse until your friend Josh stepped in. Probably saved your life, and now he's charged with attempted murder."

"Wait, wait…" Mort said. "This is more than I can comprehend. Josh is charged with attempted murder? Of who?"

"The fire marshal," Danni said. "I met Josh, and he's a fine young man. Apparently, he was in his taxi looking after you while you were sneaking around the bookstore site. Luckily, he had night vision goggles—God knows why—and saw this guy hit you with the baton. You apparently went down like the proverbial ton of bricks."

"I never saw him coming, never heard him," Mort said. "But how did Josh get involved?"

"Josh saw him getting ready to beat you again. The guy probably would have killed you—which, of course, you brought on yourself, my hero. So Josh gunned his car, horn blaring, brights on, and ran him down. Broke both his legs—but saved your bacon."

Mort put his hand over his eyes. This was almost more than he could fathom.

"So, where's the fire marshal?" Mort asked.

"The veterans hospital, whatever its official name is, with two broken legs. Femur severed on one leg, fibula and tibia in the other. Compound fractures, so he won't be in any dance competitions in the immediate future."

As the story unfolded, Cletus McNair Jr., the fire marshal, had gone back to the scene of the explosion carrying a container of liquefied ethyl mercaptan, the foul-smelling liquid he was going to spread around. He was anxious that Mort or someone else might do what Mort did—go back to the ruins to investigate further. If he spread that chemical around, Mort, or anyone else, would be thrown off. Since Cletus had already made a determination of cause and closed the investigation, he felt reasonably safe, but he decided not to take any chances.

When Cletus got to the scene and saw Mort there, he took his baton and smashed Mort over the head from behind. Clearly, he was prepared to continue the beating until he was run down by Josh's taxi.

The fire marshal figured that even if there was an investigation, he would say that he saw a trespasser inside the police tape, assumed it was a looter, and struck the offender's head with his baton. If it turned out to be a nosy reporter, so be it. He was in the clear.

"The only reason Cletus would have done that," reasoned Mort, "was to tamper with evidence and make it look like the explosion was an accident. Which I was convinced it wasn't. But he had closed the investigation, so why bother?"

"Good thinking, Sherlock," Danni said. "But it damn near got you killed."

Josh had called 911 immediately, and the fire marshal's plan unraveled. As a result of all this mayhem, Mort was removed to the hospital trauma room with a severe concussion and Cletus was taken to the veterans hospital at his insistence. The container of ethyl mercaptan fell to the ground at the scene. Josh was arrested for running the marshal down.

When he found out what was happening, Lawrence Greene had contacted the *Post* and they had contacted Danni, who immediately flew to Biloxi after dropping the twins off in Travilah. Mort had been unconscious for two days before regaining consciousness.

"That son of a bitch murdered Molly Perkins," Mort muttered. "I was convinced that was no propane accident. Molly was too smart and too careful. I'm not going to let him get away with this."

"Out of your hands," Danni said. "The FBI is on the investigation."

"How'd the feds get involved?" Mort asked.

"When we figured out what went down, Councilman Greene, the police chief and me agreed I should reach out to Katelyn Barrington, and she contacted the right people in the bureau. That got the wheels turning. Your friend the fire marshal will probably be charged with murder, plus there may be some federal civil rights crimes involved as well. The FBI analyzed liquid he was going to spread around—it was not a common chemical. There was a bombing involved, and the dead lady was a well-known Black author and activist."

Katelyn Barrington was a special agent with the FBI who had gone to law school with Danni. While Danni had sought a career in academics—she was now assistant professor at American University Law School—Katelyn had opted for government service and joined the FBI. They had reunited on Mort's assignment to North Dakota two years earlier and had kept in touch.

"But why?" Mort asked. "Cletus couldn't have been that upset because the bookstore was opening."

"If his wife was one of the movers and shakers in the local chapter of Families for Freedom—the Bible-thumping, book banning, right wing do-gooders—maybe she put him up to it. Or maybe he was just trying to curry favor."

"Shit," Mort said, "this thing has more tentacles than an octopus."

"I love when you're so articulate," Danni said sarcastically.

Mort was released from the hospital the following day but was restricted from flying for several more days because of the concussion. So, despite Danni's insistence that he avoid any exertion, he immediately got involved.

Fifteen

Mort called Marcie Gold, his managing editor, from the hotel in Biloxi.

"I guess it was only a matter of time before we had one of these conversations," she said.

"Honestly, I don't go out of my way to find these situations," Mort explained sheepishly.

"And as I told you, my brother just has stray dogs find him. So, bring me up to date. But first, how are you doing?"

"Well, obviously, I'm out of the hospital, but I can't fly for several days. I have a perpetual headache, and I feel like a fool."

"Danni still with you?"

"Yes, she's here."

"I have to meet her when you get back," Marcie said, "and offer her my condolences. She must have a strong constitution to put up with you."

"Thanks a lot. While I'm here, I want to conduct a couple more interviews with library people and find out more about this Families for Freedom organization. The fire marshal's wife is apparently involved with them up to her neck."

"It's your neck we're worried about," Marcie said. "What's your status with the police?"

"Well, I'm still charged with trespassing, but my local contact on the city council says that will go away once I'm arraigned now that the feds have stepped in. And because the bombing was apparently solved by my curiosity," Mort said.

"Solved by curiosity… or stupidity," Marcie said ironically. "The next time the DC police need a bomb sniffer, I'll have them send for you. What about the young man who brought down your attacker? What's his name again? I should remember it because we already did a story about how he saved you."

Mort rolled his eyes. Danni walked into the hotel room, so he switched to speakerphone. Putting his hand over the mic, he whispered, "I'm speaking to Marcie." She nodded and took the phone.

"Hello, Marcie. Danni here. Nice to meet you, but not necessarily like this."

"Hi, we've got to meet once you're home. I want to see what kind of woman can put up with this guy."

"Just a lot of Valium and vodka," Danni said.

"Let's do lunch when you're back," Marcie said. "I just called my predecessor, Steve Ginsberg, at the Times to tell him about Mort's latest adventure, but he had already read about it and said it was par for the course."

* * *

After finishing the call, Mort met with Josh Brown and Lawrence Greene in the coffee shop adjacent to the hotel. Josh was explaining his version of the night's events.

"Just like I listen to the police radio, I keep a pair of night vision goggles in the car," Josh explained. "When I saw him getting ready to clobber you again, I turned on the brights, hit the horn and drove into him. Never really thought about it."

"How close were you?" Mort asked. "I told you to get out of there."

"I don't listen to my mother, either," Josh said. "Let's just say I was close enough to do what had to be done. I just had the feeling that you were looking for trouble."

"And… the criminal charges?"

Lawrence Greene answered. Mort had never seen him without shorts and sandals. He was wearing a light seersucker suit with an open-necked, flowered pink shirt. Quite the dandy.

"As soon as I heard what was going down," Greene said, "I contacted the NAACP locally, where I'm well-known, and they provided an attorney—a crackerjack—and we got Josh out on his own recognizance. They reduced the attempted murder charge to assault, but that will go away once we get a full hearing. He's a local hero."

"Yeah, a hero who will probably have to move far away from here when Cletus's buddies digest it all," Josh said. "But I did get an interview and story in the Washington Post. And Mort's pictures from his cell phone." He turned to Mort and said, "Yeah, we borrowed your phone."

Greene said, "And you got a lot of positive publicity both locally and nationally. You saved a Pulitzer Prize-winning reporter. Certainly won't hurt your résumé."

"The DC area is a great place to live," Mort said. "But you might be over-reacting, Josh. After they see the reaction to the bombing by law enforcement, and with the FBI involved, I can't imagine you'll be in any jeopardy."

"That's the logical approach. But these guys are not smart or logical."

"Let's see what happens. You're always welcome to visit with us and get a taste of DC."

* * *

Three days later, Mort was back at his desk at the *Post*. He and Danni had flown from Biloxi to Jackson, where he met with the ladies from the *Jackson Free Press*, Kalie Grisholm and Donna Lublin. They had lined up several interviews with librarians and an officer from the Mississippi ACLU. Families for Freedom was not only extremely active in Jackson but had reached out to many communities in the state. They tried to exert pressure on members of the legislature to pass statewide laws restricting what people could read—especially children and teenagers. They showed up at city council and library board meetings to lobby their cause, often in disruptive fashion, intimidating and threatening local librarians. It was a well-orchestrated and organized effort not unlike those that focused on voter suppression and pro-life activities.

"It's not just here in Mississippi that this travesty is happening," said Raoul Spielman of the ACLU. "It's spreading like wildfire all over the country. Our legal staff is overwhelmed with cases even though authors' groups like PEN, the Authors' Guild, and a lot of well-known authors are getting involved. We're starting to get help from book publishers as well. But it's just not enough. We're fighting a firestorm. These people are insidious and ruthless. They've fought to ban Holocaust books, picture books, poems—even the Inauguration poem for the president by that young woman in 2020. This goes far beyond what is appropriate or inappropriate for people, especially children. It strikes at the roots of democracy and the First Amendment."

Seeing that his little speech was holding the attention of his group, Spielman continued. "In the last year, there have been attacks and attempts to ban over 4,200 books, and when we ban books, we ban knowledge, culture, education, and everything that made this country great. We really need the press to make this a priority, because it strikes at the foundation of freedom of speech."

"I'm just one voice," Mort said, "but I'll speak to my editor and see if we can't expand these stories into a series."

Mort left with a list of the states where book banning attempts seemed to be the most prevalent—Florida, Texas, Tennessee, Wisconsin and Idaho. The problem clearly was not restricted to any particular area of the country. He also was provided with a list of dozens of books that had come under attack. The federal district courts had become clogged with litigation, and in many states, librarians, people who had dedicated their lives to serving and educating their communities, were quitting their jobs in the face of the threats and intimidation.

Sixteen

Washington, DC

Mort sat facing psychologist Dr. Irwin Silverstein wearing jeans and a sweatshirt. "I'm glad you could fit me into the schedule," he said. "I go back to work tomorrow."

"I'm not used to seeing you out of your workout clothes," Silverstein said, "but I read of your exploits—both before and after you went south."

"That's just it," Mort said. "When I left you after the last session, these two young hoods were trying to carjack a woman."

"And you had to get involved instead of calling the police."

"It was a 'time is of the essence' moment."

"Doesn't that always seem to be the way with you?" Silverstein asked. "There's never time. But from what I read of your adventure in Mississippi, I believe there *was* time, but you chose to be someplace you weren't supposed to be and almost got yourself killed."

"I was convinced Molly Perkins, the author, had been murdered," Mort said. "And if I hadn't investigated, that fire marshal would have closed the case, and the truth would never have been known."

"And, as I said, you almost got killed. You were just lucky someone saw it and saved you. Now, couldn't you have called the authorities to investigate officially and in daylight? What is your compulsion to undertake these endeavors on your own?"

"I just react, I guess."

"Or, maybe you're embarrassed to ask someone to follow up on your suspicions for fear of being wrong?"

"I hadn't looked at it that way," Mort said.

"You never seem to look at it that way, isn't that so? What we have to discover is *why*?"

"I don't know," Mort said. "Maybe it's the underlying insecurity of not being right. Maybe it's just my inquisitive nature."

"Well, we've been dealing with your insecurities," Silverstein said, "like the fact that you don't feel you deserve Danni, but you never seem to accept your positives. Your intelligence, for example. Your history of success in your profession and in life in general. From what you tell me of Danni, she is not one to accept a second-rate relationship and didn't marry you out of pity. She chose you. She had other choices, just like the physician you told me she rejected years ago. And others. Doesn't that enforce your inner confidence? What is it that are you looking for?"

"I guess... well, honestly, I still don't know," Mort said. "I thought I was dead after I got hit in the head, and then she came flying out to be by my side. Left the twins and was there in a day."

"Doesn't that enforce your self-confidence? Doesn't that tell you something?"

"It tells me that she cares, yes. I know she loves me. Yet, somehow I'm compelled to act in these situations."

"And you end up getting favorable publicity as a reward. You end up being labeled a hero. Again. You end up solving crimes. Is the need for acceptance, appreciation, accolades—is that part of it?"

"That's what I'm here to find out. What do *you* think?"

"No," Silverstein said, "you've got to find the answers. What we are doing is searching your inner self. Introspection. Questioning your motives. That's where the answers lie."

After a few more minutes, they adjourned until Mort's next scheduled session.

* * *

Early the following morning, Mort was going through his mail, his emails, and generally catching up on work when his phone rang. It was Alison. He had already heard from his prior boss, Steve Ginsberg, now with the *New York Times*.

"Mort," Alison said, "I'm glad you're still in one piece."

"He hit me in the head," Mort said, "my least critical area. How are you doing out there in Kansas? I just read your proposed two articles. When will you be back here?"

"Marcie gave me a couple more days," Alison said. "That police chief has been ducking me. But I've finally got that interview set for later today."

Mort heard a man's voice in the background say, "Just about ready?" He looked at his watch. It was only eight-thirty. That meant it was at least an hour earlier in Kansas.

"Who was that?" Mort asked.

"That was Atticus," Alison said. "He's opened a lot of doors for me."

Including, Mort thought, *your bedroom door as well.*

"Atticus?" Mort said.

"I'm seeing him," Alison said. "We're sort of quickly… uh, involved. That was the bonus from my assignment." Mort knew Alison well enough that she just wouldn't hop into bed with an almost total stranger. She had been in Kansas for almost a week. He thought back to his initial connection with Danni. On his part, it hadn't taken take long to recognize something special.

Mort smiled. "Wow. That *was* quick, but good for you. You deserve it. You can bring me up to date when you're back here."

Seventeen

In the kitchen of his condo, Atticus set two cups on the center island where two stools sat side by side. The room was painted in a soft gray, with cabinets in a soothing lime green. He was pouring coffee into the cups as Alison walked in.

"What's on the agenda for today?" he asked.

"Interview with Janice Marquette at the Shelter Rock Public Library. She went to pieces when I told her of Margery Robbins's death, so we'll sit down today. She's got another woman she wants me to interview—Stella Hobbs, the first-grade teacher who got fired when she led her class in singing Rainbow Connection from the Muppets."

"She teaches in our other grammar school," Atticus said. "Hard to believe that Kermit the Frog offends these folks. That was another endeavor led by my ex-wife. Everything that turns to shit around here seems to have her hand in it. I know that the ACLU got Hobbs a lawyer, and hopefully she'll be back in class by the time we resume in August."

"I meant to ask you about that," Alison said. "If school is out for the summer, how come you had your whole class at the museum the other day?"

"At the end of each year, I give them a field trip, this year a museum tour," Atticus explained. "A bonus for not bringing any loaded guns to class all year—just kidding—a way to say farewell until fall."

"What a nice gesture," Alison said. "I could tell how much they liked you."

"Don't know about that, but my end of year bonus was meeting you that day. It's the best thing that's happened to me. I think it changed my life."

"Let's not get too far ahead of ourselves," Alison said. "But these few days have certainly been incredible. Then I'll be back in DC, and you'll be here, halfway across the country, and while I don't want this—whatever *this* is—to end, let's be realistic."

"Have plane, will travel," Atticus said. "I'm not letting you get away that easily." He reached over and kissed her, and she responded warmly.

As they separated, Alison said, "I finally got an interview with that police chief of yours, Val Cummings, which should be very interesting."

"Watch that one. He's a worm."

"Well, with the extra time I had here, I was able to do some checking on him with a friend in Omaha, and I think he could be in for a few surprises if I need them. And then I'll be finished here and ready to head back to the paper. I planned to attend the bi-weekly city council meeting, but they postponed it—I think because they knew I was coming. I inquired but didn't get a warm welcome. Your local prosecutor, the one who originally sought the search warrant for the Clarion on the flimsiest of evidence, is 'unavailable' to discuss the case because there may be litigation. And the judge, as you know, suddenly took a vacation. Bottom line, I have a flight out on American at eleven tomorrow morning."

"You're really leaving me then?" Atticus wiped away an imaginary tear.

"I have to leave by seven to return the rental," Alison said.

"Tell you what. You can leave the rental here. I'll turn it in, and I'll fly you to KC in the morning. Better than a two- or three-hour drive. How's that for service? The big question is—when will I see you again?"

"We'll work on that."

She thought about what had brought Atticus into her life—the raid on a local newspaper. And that had led to stumbling on some information that would help Mort on the book banning article. And it had also led to Atticus entering her life. Funny how things happen.

* * *

Janice Marquette was waiting for Alison at the library, wearing her librarian's smock and her outlandish, multi-colored sneakers. With her was a pony-tailed, young blond woman whom she introduced as Stella Hobbs. Wearing a sleeveless blouse, jeans and sockless loafers, Hobbs looked more like a college student than a grammar school teacher. She had only been teaching one year prior to her firing by the school board.

"I never even gave a thought that the song Rainbow Connection could be offensive to anyone," Hobbs said. "We grew up with Sesame Street, Kermit and the whole crew. What is this world coming to if a song about rainbows is offensive because it allegedly emphasizes the LBGTQ way of life? Which, of course, it doesn't. But they never even gave me a chance to explain. Said I was trying to foist my 'doctrine' on the kids. I'm single, but I'm not gay. Not that anyone asked. It's a pleasant and fun song, that's all."

"So much for Somewhere Over the Rainbow," Alison said. "Judy Garland must be turning over in her grave. There must be dozens of songs about rainbows."

"My attorney did some research," Hobbs said. "Came up with over seventy—and that's just in the title. Elvis Presley, Dolly Parton, Louis Armstrong—all well-known for their gay philosophies, right?"

Alison said, "It may be ludicrous, but it will certainly add some spice to my articles."

Hobbs explained that the firing came near the end of the school year. The attorney from the ACLU was taking the case pro bono—without a fee—having docketed it in the federal district court. They hoped to have a decision, a favorable one, before the summer was over.

The school board, following the lead of "Save Shelter Rock," a Christian-based nonprofit headed by Tish Duvall, Atticus's ex-wife, challenged over five hundred book titles on the shelves of the schools within the district. All had been removed. The library board, challenged by the same group, threatened to fire librarians who did not adhere to their mandates. It also threatened to defund or close libraries and prosecute librarians for distributing books on their banned lists. Save Shelter Rock was the local affiliate of Families for Freedom. They had even attacked a book about two rabbits holding each other's paws, as encouraging homosexuality.

Janice Marquette said, "You can see what we have to put up with. It's ludicrous, it's stifling education, it tramples on free speech and…" she paused, "…it's not indicative of the will of the majority. The Clarion has been filled with angry letters to the editor opposing book banning and opposing Stella's firing. And Margery wrote a powerful editorial only a few weeks before she died. The kids even walked out of class after Stella was fired—imagine, little tykes protesting—and that set some hair afire around here."

The three women were seated at a table in the middle of the library. Alison had her laptop open and was taking notes. The library was open, and at least one woman stared at the three of them before she walked out.

"That's Glenda Bigelow," Janice Marquette said with disgust. "Should be named Glenda Big Mouth, really. She just checked us out, and she'll be running to Tish Duvall of the Conscience Police to turn us in."

"Is that Atticus's ex-wife?" Alison asked.

"None other," Janice Marquette said. "Now *that* was a union straight from hell. Best thing that ever happened to him was getting rid of her."

Alison shifted uncomfortably in her chair. "I've been spending time with Atticus while I was here," she said, blushing.

"Oh, don't think it hasn't been noticed since you were with him at the funeral," Janice Marquette said. "There's no way Tish didn't spot that."

"Oh, she did, for sure," Alison said.

"Well, unless you were also selling drugs or dealing in cocaine, you're probably safe," Hobbs added.

Janice Marquette said, "Getting back to why you were sent out here, where does all this go from here? You can use Stella's name, because that story is all over, and they know the way I feel about this, so the worst they can do is fire me, too, and engender more bad publicity. And I'm not losing sleep over it. I've been a fixture in this community for thirty-five years, and I've got my retirement and even Social Security if I need it. I'm not afraid to speak up, and there are some of those do-gooders who are actually intimidated by me. Plus, so many people spoke out after Stella was fired, and now, with the ACLU involved, they're holding their fire until they see the outcome of the case."

Alison explained that the reason she was sent to Shelter Rock was to investigate the raid on the *Clarion*, censorship, and the attempt to stifle the voice of the paper. The book banning, and subjects like Stella Hobbs's firing were actually something that her boss, Mort Ahrens, was working on. She would report what she found in Shelter Rock and await a decision on where it would go from there.

"The only other thing on my agenda before I head back to DC," Alison said, "is to interview the police chief, Val Cummings. Everyone else has ducked out on me, even the judge and the city council."

"Watch your step with that one," Hobbs said. "He's a misogynist pig. He even came on to me, and I'm young enough to be his daughter."

"To be forewarned is to be forearmed," Alison said, "and you're not alone in that evaluation."

Eighteen

Val Cummings was an imposing six-foot-five, fiftyish man who wore his hair long and had a .45 slung low on his hip. His officers wore peaked caps while he wore a black Cattleman cowboy hat with a deep center crease, doing his best to emulate a Texas Ranger. On his beige tunic, a gold star glistened. He had a cleft chin, deep-set, dark eyes and a deceiving smile that revealed gleaming white teeth.

He met Alison at the entrance to the police station on North Fifth Street. His cruiser bearing the city emblem and embellished with "Chief" was parked at the entrance to the one-story building. He greeted Alison by clasping both her hands warmly and hung onto them long enough to make her uncomfortable. "So, you're with the Washington Post. Tell me, are all your reporters this hot?"

"Only when we're in the Kansas heat," Alison answered crisply.

"Good one," Cummings said. "Let's go inside, and then you can feel free to attack me."

"I really just want an interview. And I appreciate your agreeing, because everyone else seems to be unavailable or on vacation."

"A bunch of pussies," Cummings said.

They walked into the building. The offices were plain and unadorned, with an Ikea table against the back wall covered with bags of what appeared to be confiscated marijuana and other drugs. A dog bed sat on the floor next to it."

"Tillie's bed," Cummings said.

"Oh, and was she part of the raid on the Clarion? In case any of the lady reporters got out of hand?" Alison said.

Cummings put back his head and laughed. "Oh, I see you're a feisty one. I like that in a woman. Let's go into my office where it's cooler and we can be more comfortable." He reached out and put his arm around her waist, guiding her into his office. She stiffened as his motion felt more like a caress than a steering.

"What I'm here for is merely the facts about the raid," she said, pulling away.

"I've got nothing to hide," Cummings said, as if he hadn't noticed. "I just carry out the directions of the city fathers, the judge and law enforcement, and try to keep the peace."

They sat down in two chairs facing his desk. As she looked around, she noticed a large flag on the wall facing his desk. It had the thirteen stripes of an American flag, but in the blue square were thirteen white stars in a circular fashion with three white, single Roman numerals displayed prominently in the middle. Alison immediately recognized the design.

"You're a Three-Percenter?" she said in disbelief.

"They dissolved in 2021," Cummings said uncomfortably. "This is just sort of a memento."

"But you were a member?"

"Advocates for gun rights, gun ownership," Cummings said.

"And advocates for resistance to our government," Alison responded.

"Long in the past," Cummings said. "Only thing I got out of it was that souvenir. It's a collector's item."

Alison stared at him. She was wearing slacks and a soft blouse that draped over her breasts. She noticed his eyes focused, uncomfortably for her, on her breasts. After the surprise of seeing the flag, she groped for something to say.

"My first reaction is that you remind me of someone. *I know!* You remind me of my father," Alison said, trying to divert his attention.

"Thanks a lot," Cummings replied dryly.

"Do you like baseball?" she asked.

Surprised by the question, Cummings said, "Love baseball. Still play a little. Do you *play*?" The way he said "play" almost had a sexual connotation.

"I don't," Alison replied, "but that approach is not going to get you as far as first base with me. So, let's just concentrate on the interview."

"It never hurts to try. Atticus Duvall seems to have scored favorably, I hear."

"Is there anything that goes on around here that is not public knowledge?" Alison asked with a sharp tone. She shook her head in disgust and then continued. "I just met the man. Let's get down to business. You have a department of four officers and yet there was a half dozen of you on the raid on the Clarion. Did you have to ask for help from another city?"

Alison already knew the answer from her previous research, but she wanted to see his reaction.

"Nothing happens here that I can't control. I used some of my part-time deputies. Couldn't leave the city undefended."

"And what led you to seize all of their equipment, down to cell phones and material on the desks?"

"The warrant was very specific," Cummings said. "Search and *seizure*. So, we seized, just like the warrant told us to. Remember, it was requested by the prosecutor and signed by the judge. I don't have discretion. I just follow legal directives."

"Legal?" Alison said. "What about the First Amendment? Freedom of the press? Couldn't you have questioned it? What possibly could have triggered this? Was the Clarion running an illegal operation? Are they a crime family? This was not just a search. You almost shut them down."

"As I said," Cummings replied, "my job is to carry out legal mandates, and that's what we did. Granted that the Clarion is not the most popular business in town. Seems to do an uncommon amount of prying, if you know what I mean. You know, there's exceptions to the law if newspapers or reporters are committing a crime."

"But there was no crime committed by the Clarion. Or am I wrong? They never published the information about that ancient drunk driving arrest. And if they had, it was truthful and they had a right to publish it. The bottom line is, that information was public and available to anyone. It was all in the public record. And that's *your* law."

Cummings squirmed in his chair, perhaps not used to being confronted so directly by a woman.

Alison continued. "I think the Clarion did the job of a good newspaper. In addition, I saw the warrant, and it didn't say anything about seizing cell phones. And certainly not yanking one out of a woman's hand so harshly that it broke a finger."

"Maybe one of the boys got overzealous, but she shouldn't have resisted. The warrant said 'communications equipment.' Far as I know, you use cell phones to communicate. We did everything by the book."

"Apparently, Shelter Rock has a unique book. According to what I saw, the prosecutor requested this warrant because he suspected the Clarion had illegally obtained the driving record of a citizen from unprotected information available to anyone. How on earth would that lead to a raid like the one you conducted? And didn't that Clarion employee who had her finger broken already sue you?"

"Not really me, but the police department, yes. And that's why we have very expensive insurance coverage."

"But how do you equate what happened with probable cause?"

Cummings lifted his hands, palms up, as if to say, search me, I don't know, and then said, "Better ask the prosecutor. Or the judge."

"Unavailable, and out of town. Conveniently," Alison said. "Do you have anything more to add that I haven't covered?"

"Not unless you'd like to join me for a drink," Cummings said. "I don't drink during duty hours, but for you, I'm willing to make an exception."

"Duly noted, and I'll pass," Alison said. "Thank you for your time."

"Just make sure you spell the name right," Cummings said smugly. "I've had a long career in law enforcement."

"Oh, I know," Alison said, with a smile. "I've followed your career from Omaha and beyond, so why don't we leave it at that."

Cummings's attitude changed markedly, and his expression darkened as she rose and walked out.

Nineteen

Alison, seated with Mort in his cubicle, was going over copies of the day's *Washington Post* when Marcie Gold appeared.

"Alison, really good work," Marcie said. "You managed to ferret out information none of the other media outlets carried. How did you manage that?"

"Probably the unfortunate death of Margery Robbins, and my getting stuck there a couple of additional days," Alison said. "I made some contacts that I wouldn't have made on a quick in-and-out."

"As I read your articles, seems this all boiled up because that hotel owner discovered the paper had gained access to her old drunk driving arrest and was afraid it'd stop her license renewal," Marcie said.

"Yes, they got a tip about the old arrest," Alison said. "But that information probably wouldn't have stopped the renewal. It was not secret and it was a few decades old. But she got paranoid, went to her buddies, and that led to the raid on the Clarion."

"How the hell did that result in a search warrant?"

"I took the temperature of Shelter Rock," Alison said. "It's boiling hot. Almost incestuous. Even though the woman was rumored to be a disliked drunk, it gave the city an opportunity to shut down the paper they hated, so they tried, First Amendment be damned. The townsfolk certainly reacted. Her restaurant in the hotel is like a morgue."

"Why did they hate the paper?"

"Margery ruffled a lot of feathers with her columns. This gave them an opportunity to stifle her. The mayor, the city council, the local prosecutor, even the judge had felt the sting of her barbed words and investigations. All of which were well deserved by the way."

"So this woman recruited a circle of collaborators to take down the Clarion?"

"The prosecutor, who is a cousin of the judge, who disappeared when I started inquiring about her, made up this phony request for a search warrant on very tenuous grounds. Everyone signed off. The sad thing is that it was apparently more than Margery, who was almost a hundred years old, could take—especially when they raided her at home and confiscated all her equipment. Margery was restricted to a walker and screamed to no avail. She died the night I got there."

"Well," Marcie said, "keep it going. We got a lot of positive feedback from outfits like PEN and the Writers Guild and names like Grisham and Turow. It was blockbuster work."

At this point, Mort interjected, "Boss, that's one of the things we were just discussing."

"Boss?" Marcie said. "Since when have I become 'Boss?' You make me sound like an old lady."

Mort smiled. "No offense, just deference to your position. Anyway, in working on the censorship story, Alison has uncovered a lot of leads into the book banning piece I'm putting together. Apparently, this little city in Kansas has some deep roots in Families for Freedom, and I found a local outfit called Clean Up Biloxi in Mississippi, which is apparently a local affiliate. It may spread far beyond what we originally imagined. This is going to require a lot of digging."

"Well," Marcie said, "maybe both of you should work together once Alison has milked the censorship bit. We'll authorize whatever you need."

"And my vacation?" Mort moaned.

"Secure and guaranteed," Marcie said. "But first things first."

"Danni may seek a divorce."

"Oh, yes," Marcie said. "That's one of the things I was going to tell you. We're meeting for lunch in a few days. I'll soften the blow."

Mort sagged in his chair and put his hand over his eyes.

* * *

Alison was back at her desk when her phone rang. It was a number she didn't recognize.

"Alison Powers," she said.

"Alison, this is Janice Marquette in Shelter Rock, and I thought you should know. Atticus is in jail."

"In jail?" Alison shouted. "For what? When? What happened?"

"The police chief charged him with disorderly conduct," Janice Marquette said. "He and Atticus argued and it apparently got loud, so Cummings slapped the cuffs on him and put him in the clink. He goes to court tomorrow."

"Disorderly conduct? I don't understand," Alison said.

"From what I know, Atticus was in the barbershop getting a haircut when Cummings walked in and said something sarcastic about his relationship with you. Atticus reacted, jumped out of the chair and told Cummings what he thought of him in less than courteous language. Apparently, he was close to hauling off, so Cummings arrested him."

"I don't believe this," Alison said. "Sounds like the Keystone Kops."

"Is there anything I can do?" Janice Marquette asked. "He'll for sure be released tomorrow."

"He'll be released before tomorrow if I have anything to do with it, so please stand by," Alison said. "And Janice, thank you. I'll take it from here."

Alison still had Cummings's personal phone number, so she called and he picked up.

"I was wondering how quickly I'd hear from you, pretty lady," Cummings said.

Alison said, "You listen to me, Val." She hadn't called him that before. "I will say this only once, so listen carefully, and unless you give me an unqualified 'yes,' I will be on the phone with Eric Robbins the minute I hang up."

"And why would I do that?" Cummings said in an artificially sweet tone.

"Because I did a lot of checking up on you from sources in Omaha," Alison said, "which I never mentioned or used. I'm sure you remember Omaha. A captain there suddenly resigned, took his pension and moved to a little city in Kansas where he now earns one-quarter of what he was earning in the big city."

"I needed less stress," Cummings said.

"What you needed," Alison said forcefully, "was to get out of Omaha to escape two charges of sexual harassment that were lodged against you. One with an under-age female. They let you get out of town to save the department's reputation, and to save the city a boatload of money from the lawsuits. And don't think those non-disclosure agreements these women signed will help you. I have statements from both women, and that underage girl was not competent to sign her NDA. What do you think, Groping Gus?"

"I think that you're overreacting. Besides, how do I know I can trust you?" Cummings said.

"Because I have integrity," Alison said, "a word you wouldn't understand."

"What do you want me to do?"

"Drop the charges and immediately release Atticus. Say it was a misunderstanding and it all goes away. And I mean do it NOW!" Alison shouted the last word.

"Boy, he must really have conned you, or whatever," Cummings said. "Or else he's hung like a—"

"Don't say it," Alison interrupted, "or I'll hang up now and call Eric. What a juicy story for the Clarion. And maybe even the Post since its connected to the series we're now publishing. I can see the headline now—'Police Chief Lied on Application. Multiple sexual harassment charges in Omaha.'"

There was a long silence before Cummings said, "Okay, you win. He'll be out as soon as I sign the papers."

Alison smiled to herself. She didn't really have statements from the women in Omaha.

A half hour later, Alison looked down at a caller's number on her phone. It was Atticus.

"I'm here with Janice," he said, "down the street from police headquarters. What the hell did you do? He was as meek as a lamb."

"All in a day's work," Alison said. "Nothing more to discuss. I may be seeing you soon. And you'll get a chance to meet Mort as well."

"I can't wait," Atticus said.

Twenty

Mort was staring at two piles of clippings on his desk when Alison burst in. He had earphones on and was humming "Mamas, Don't Let Your Babies Grow Up to be Cowboys". He pushed the earphones back, pointed to the piles and said, "I've been printing out stories about book banning—from legislatures, to libraries, to city councils and library boards, as well as individual stories from all over the country. This thing is much bigger than we realized. Over four thousand attacks on books in the last year. And some violence too. Once we—"

Alison interrupted, her face flushed and hands wildly flapping. "You won't believe what that son of a bitch police chief just tried to get away with in Kansas."

She sat down and related the story to Mort. When she finished, he leaned back and laughed.

She was miffed. "I don't think it's funny."

"But he fell for it. Thought you had statements from the women."

"Yeah, but the sexual harassment story is true," Alison said, "and I wasn't about to use it until he threw Atticus into the clink. But I didn't have statements, no."

"Good for you, that was a stroke of genius," Mort said. "I have to meet this Atticus. You and he must really have hit it off to get that kind of a rise out of the police chief. Or did you two take out an ad in the Clarion?"

"Very funny. No, Atticus is a great guy. You'll see."

"I can't wait. *Now…* as I was saying when you walked in… we can split up all this research, boil it down into notes and bullet points, and figure out a plan of action."

* * *

The phone on Mort's desk started vibrating. He had the ringer turned off because when he was concentrating, particularly when writing a story, it broke his train of thought. He picked up the phone and said, "Mort Ahrens."

"Mort, Devin Leo in Jackson."

"Devin, good to hear from you. I hope to be seeing you folks shortly as we dig deeper into these book banning situations."

"Well," Devin said, "I thought that you should know. Irene Diamond, the lawyer from the case you sat in on, was mugged and killed last night."

Mort gasped. "My God, isn't anyone safe down there anymore?"

"It's worse than that," Devin said. "Seems to be linked to her representing the librarian in that case."

"Linked? In what way?"

"She was stabbed, and a Bible was left on her body with a note calling her a heathen."

"Holy shit!" Mort exclaimed. "This thing is getting insane. Are the police certain about this? That it wasn't just some lunatic or client with a grudge?"

"The FBI is on it already," Devin said. "They're treating it as a hate crime. Or at least investigating it as one. But we thought you should know. Kalie and Donna are distraught because they had recommended her as the lawyer."

"I can understand that," Mort said. "Send them my condolences. And tell them to keep looking over their shoulder. This is way beyond the bizarre. How old was she? Married? Kids? This is just crazy."

"She was thirty-eight and divorced. Two young kids," Devin said.

Mort shook his head. There was nothing he could do.

After a few more words, Devin hung up, and Mort sat back in his chair, eyes closed but thinking silently. So far, since he'd accepted this assignment, there had been three deaths in a few short weeks. First it was Margery Robbins who had died a day after the police raid on her newspaper and home, and now this lawyer representing a woman in a civil case about book banning who probably took the case without even charging a fee. And also, there was Molly Perkins, the author who was undoubtedly murdered in a bookstore explosion.

These deaths were completely different and miles apart in different states. There couldn't be any connection. Or could there?

It wouldn't be the first time that Mort's fertile imagination had created weird scenarios in his mind. He remembered that as a kid at night he would come up with crazy thoughts where his mind imagined all sorts of conspiracies and devious plots and schemes. They amounted to nothing more than his imagination working overtime. Was this just another example of that? He often felt that these imaginative leaps had somehow led to his becoming a journalist. *Something to discuss with Danni, or more appropriately, with Irwin Silverstein,* he thought, before he snapped back to the material on his desk and the matter at hand.

Twenty-one

Travilah, Maryland

Sitting around the dining room table at J.J.'s and Chickie's on a warm summer evening, Danni and Mort were relaxing as Lupe hovered over the twins and fed them ice cream. The four adults at the table were also having ice cream, and conversing. Mort and Danni's springer spaniel, Katie, sniffed at the foot of the highchairs, waiting for some ice cream to drop.

"Mom and I have been talking," Danni said, "and—"

"Uh oh," Mort interrupted.

"Here comes trouble," J.J. said, "because whenever the two of you are talking, there's a plot afoot."

"No, no plot," Danni said. "Just an idea. A good idea."

Chickie and J.J. had now been married for more than four years. While Chickie was still the CEO of the media conglomerate she took over when her husband had died, she now spent a lot of time with J.J. when the Supreme Court was recessed for the summer. J.J., who was a childless widower when he was introduced to Chickie by Danni, doted on the twins, his only grandchildren. Unlike some of his brethren on the court, he eschewed perks and free trips and wouldn't consider anything more than an occasional speaking engagement for which he never accepted an honorarium. Now in his eighties, he still enjoyed his annual Law and Order end-of-the-season speaking engagement at Winston Churchill High School in Potomac, Maryland, with good friend and now Supreme Court Police Chief Travis Anderson. He also relished his Labor Day barbeques for fellow justices and court personnel.

"Anyhow, as I was saying before my husband rudely interrupted me as usual," Danni continued, "Mom and I said that since our vacations are so routinely interfered with, by Mort's schedule, to say nothing of our honeymoon, and since he's about to embark on this multi-cities tour for his book banning story, maybe we could leave the twins with you guys for a few days and I could go with him. I'm not teaching this summer, and it would give us some well-needed together time."

"We'd love that," Chickie said.

"Finally, a suggestion that would be great for everybody," J.J. said. "Sounds like a plan."

"Sí, now for sure I teach the babies Spanish," Lupe interjected.

Mort joked, "As long as Dakota doesn't call me amigo before he learns to say daddy."

"Are they too young to learn on the Harley?" J.J. asked.

"They're too young, you're too old, and one of the best things I ever did was making you sell the damn thing," Chickie said. "How long will you be gone, Mort?"

"A week, ten days at most," Mort said. "We'll do Mississippi, Kansas and several other southern states where these book banners and Families for Freedom seem to be well entrenched. They're cropping up like mosquitos everywhere, which is what I'm working on. It will probably end up as a series of articles. Violence is now accompanying this weird movement as well. One librarian's attorney I met was killed this week, though they haven't solved that case yet. But I have my suspicions."

"We? Did you say we?" Danni said.

"Oh, I guess I didn't mention that Alison is going along on this trip," Mort said sheepishly.

"Now I'm *definitely* going," Danni said.

Mort smiled and said, "No worries. She seems to have a significant other. Kind of sudden... a guy named Atticus in Kansas.

Must have made a terrific impression on her, and she's not easy to impress, because they were only together a week or so. She just got him out of jail."

"Sounds like a great way to start a relationship," Chickie said.

Mort related the story of Alison's episode in Kansas, and they talked a bit before Mort and Danni packed up the twins and Katie and headed back home to DC.

* * *

With the twins asleep in their cribs, Mort and Danni were preparing for bed and discussing his assignment. Mort was practicing some of his Krav Maga moves in his shorts while Danni watched, amused.

"This Families for Freedom organization seems to have branches everywhere," Mort said. "And they're threatening libraries, library boards, town and city councils. They're getting more militant as they get more powerful. There are more than a hundred thousand members nationally. I've really got to get an inside track to them."

"Why not have someone join?" Danni said.

"I wouldn't want anyone to carry that stigma," Mort said.

Danni was silent for about half a minute, then said, "How about getting Katie to join?"

"A dog? I don't think they're taking dogs, and I'm being unfair to dogs in that comparison."

"No—as a ruse," Danni said. "We create a website for Katie—KatieSpringer.com or something—and have her join. Her name *is* Katie, and she *is* a Springer. Then you can get an inside track on them."

Mort stopped in the middle of one of his moves. "You're a genius," he said. "I knew there was a reason I married you."

Danni swatted at him with an open hand, and he grabbed her arm and pulled her into him.

Twenty-two

The drone of the airplane engines was making Danni's eyes heavy. Across the aisle, Alison was already dozing with a large man seated next to her fixated on the screen in front of him. Mort glanced at his two companions and smiled. He could rarely sleep on planes and found that it was a good time to prepare for a coming assignment, which he was doing. He had a stack of printouts on his lap, information he had copied from the morgue at the *Post*. Mort insisted on referring to it as "the morgue," although the vernacular had changed, and the politically correct term now was "the library" or "the archive."

Danni fished a set of ear buds out of her purse, leaned back and closed her eyes.

"What are you listening to?" Mort asked.

"Vivaldi, The Four Seasons, which will lull me right to sleep," she replied. Their taste in music was markedly different.

Mort said, "This organization, Families for Freedom, is really amazing. And I don't mean that in a good way. They only started four years ago and already have members trying to ban books in practically every state."

No response. Danni was already dozing.

Mort took a tissue and wiped his glasses, smiling to himself. He looked at the beautiful woman sleeping next to him and again wondered how he had been lucky enough to end up marrying her. He thought back to their first meeting in Syracuse. As features editor for the *Daily Orange*, the student newspaper, he had been scheduled to meet the All-

American point guard who was getting national attention leading the women's team to the best season the Orange had ever enjoyed. A five-foot-two point guard. And she had managed to accomplish this while still being one of the top students in her law school class.

Danni was graduating that year, Mort was a junior undergraduate, and they had met on Marshall Street after she finished practice and before she met with her study group. They got to talking, and even though the din around them was disconcerting, they connected, until she realized she had to leave—before he got the interview. In a massive show of courage for Mort, he invited her to dinner in his apartment on Euclid Avenue the following evening. To his amazement, she accepted. If nothing else, he knew he was a good cook.

One would never have guessed that Danni's family owned a media conglomerate, because she had no airs about her. Mort's middle-class upbringing in Harrisburg was, in his eyes, nondescript, except for winning Teen Jeopardy eleven days in a row, which earned him a cash stipend large enough to pay off his parents' mortgage and still leave him with a tidy bankroll. But a relationship with Danni was more than he could have imagined. It was still a constant source of discussion with his shrink.

Danni and he drifted in and out of each other's lives after that as she began several stints as a law clerk to two federal judges and then ended up with a most sought after clerkship with J.J. Richter, the Senior Associate Justice and curmudgeon of the US Supreme Court, an avowed progressive.

In his senior year, Mort went on to a part-time job with the Syracuse *Post-Standard*, ended up being sent to cover a young woman's disappearance when no other reporters were available, followed his instincts for two weeks, and figured out that she was kidnapped and being held prisoner by a psychotic. The police did the rest. He got national coverage and ended up being offered the job with the *Washington Post* where he was now a group leader.

Mort leaned over and kissed Danni softly. She murmured, smiled, and reached a hand to his cheek. It was only a short time later that they landed in Jackson, Mississippi. They were met by Devin Leo, who drove them to the offices of the *Jackson Free Press*, where Kalie Grisholm and Donna Lublin awaited them.

"What's the latest on that attorney's murder?" Mort asked in the car.

"Still unsolved, but the police are 'working on leads' as they say. That woman was stabbed really bad," Devin said.

After introductions at the newspaper office, they all sat around a conference table and discussed their trip, the murder, and the bizarre fact that a Bible was left on the body with a sign saying "Heathen." The word "heathen" struck Mort as unusual.

"It should be a solvable crime," Mort said. "Did they check out Families for Freedom?"

"They're nuts," Lublin said. "But murder is not their style. That's for their sycophants. It could have been a crazed vagrant who read about the trial, is what the police are saying."

"The husband of the complainant was pretty hysterical," Mort said, "to the point of being threatened by the judge."

"Checked, and he had an alibi," Grisholm said.

"And the mother—the woman who made the complaint?"

"She was apparently with her son. So, they're still looking."

"FBI?"

"Not enough to prove a hate crime," Grisholm replied.

"What're the chances of me getting to talk to the police chief?" Mort asked.

"Mort, please don't get yourself involved again," Danni pleaded.

"I just had some thoughts," Mort said, "and a little talking doesn't hurt."

Danni literally threw up her hands and turned to the others. "This is what I have to live with. A little talking inevitably ends with a big involvement. Every time."

"Well, one of his hunches saved my life," Alison said, chiming in.

The two women from the newspaper looked at her, wide-eyed.

"I promise, just a short talk," Mort said. "And then we'll get to what we came out here for."

* * *

Mort got his wish and met Police Chief Joseph Kinkade, a thirty-year veteran with the force. An imposing man, he was a head taller and a hundred pounds heavier than Mort. He shook Mort's hand warmly.

"Don't tell me the Washington Post sent you all the way out here to cover this murder?" Kinkade said.

Mort explained, "No, no, I was here on another matter during the trial where Irene Diamond represented the librarian, the one that involved Mrs. Abernathy and the book banning."

"Read about that one," Kinkade said. "Lawyer apparently did a good job. But we haven't come up with anything concrete yet. By the way, I don't normally talk one on one with news people, but I've known Kalie Grisholm forever, and she gave me some impressive background on you."

"I appreciate that," Mort said, uncomfortable with the praise. "But I was just curious. When your forensics people dusted the Bible for prints, I assume it was clean."

"You assume right. Both the Bible and the note. We came up empty. We already disclosed that, so I'm not imparting anything confidential."

"Wouldn't expect you to. What about the contents of the Bible, the inside pages?" Mort asked.

"Don't know, and that's highly unlikely, but let's find out right now," Kinkade said, picking up his phone. He had a short conversation with someone and then turned to Mort. "Not the inside pages, other than the cover inside and out. Why do you ask?"

"Just a hunch. But have them dust the page where you find Mark chapter 15 verses 21 to 41."

Kinkade picked up his phone and made another call. While they waited for a response, he showed Mort around the building. As they were talking with several of the detectives, Chief Kinkade's cell phone rang. He answered, then after a long pause, said, "I'll be damned," and turned to Mort. "How the hell did you know?" he said in disbelief. "The Abernathy woman's prints, which we took as a regular part of the investigation, are all over those pages."

Mort nodded and replied, "Like I said, just a hunch. She quoted from Mark in the trial and practically recited some of it by rote. She's ultra-religious and apparently sought her vengeance on that poor attorney for making her look like a fool. Probably wiped the cover clean, but never thought about her favorite pages, the ones she quoted. She used the word 'heathen' in her testimony, and the same unusual word was found on the body. Her son, by the way, is a good kid completely cowed by her and would say anything to protect her. That alibi will unravel."

"By God, we'll make the arrest immediately. You saved us a ton of frustration. You solved a virtually unsolvable case."

"Glad my hunch paid off," Mort said. "At least justice can be done, but it won't bring that woman back to her two kids. She died for doing a good job."

* * *

Sitting around the same conference table, the four ladies were having iced tea when Mort arrived from the police station.

"And did you satisfy yourself that all is in order?" Danni asked.

"I think they've solved the case," Mort said casually.

The women looked at him intently.

"They've got the killer?" Donna Lublin said. "What happened?"

"Great police work," Mort said. "Any more iced tea around? I'm parched."

A woman employee of the paper poked her head into the room and said, "Ms. Grisholm, call for you."

Kalie got up and exited, Donna found a glass and poured some tea for Mort, and the room went silent for a moment until Kalie Grisholm burst back in and exclaimed, "Mort! That was the chief. He said you solved the murder for them! Why didn't you say something?"

Mort, sheepish and self-effacing, stirred his tea and said, "I just had a hunch and it worked out, apparently. I asked the chief to keep me out of it. Let the police take all the credit. I guess I failed in that one."

Danni said, "I don't believe it. I really owe you one. Now, explain please."

"Yes, please," Alison said.

Mort then told them of his suspicions about the Abernathy woman and her quoting of scripture during the trial, and the unusual repetition

113

of the word "heathen." He said, "She didn't even know what was in The Catcher in the Rye. She was being used—a perfect example of the story Alison and I are working on. You get these religious zealots, and they can be led by the nose. That's why this cult, which masquerades as do-gooders, is so dangerous. Such a threat to the things and the beliefs that most of us stand for."

"Well, you certainly lived up to your billing," Donna Lublin said. "This will make for a great but sad story. And I'm sure that Families for Freedom will disclaim any responsibility."

"The real guilty ones walk free," Danni said. "Where have I heard that before?"

Alison chimed in, "This just makes the mission of our story more important than ever."

Danni walked to Mort and put her hand on his shoulder. "My husband, *infallible* husband, scores once again," she said, and squeezed his shoulder.

Twenty-three

Shelter Rock, Kansas - five days later

Before they left Jackson, Mort and Alison decided they would split up their travels to the other cities that they wanted to cover for their articles. They had already amassed a great amount of printed material, but they needed first person interviews to tie it all together. They started making contacts in the cities they wanted to visit, first to newspapers to see if there were reporters or executives willing to help them, then to organizations which had been fighting book banning efforts in those places. They would then meet in Shelter Rock to allow Alison time to do a final follow-up story on the censorship article involving the *Clarion*, if warranted. That would give Mort a chance to meet with Eric Robbins of the *Clarion* and for Alison to spend a day with Atticus.

"I never realized, as we were researching the problem," Alison said, "that there were so many people and organizations mobilized against book banning. Not just newspaper editorials, parents and teachers' groups, but writers, publishers, the American Library Association—it's overwhelming."

"And comforting," Mort agreed. "They're probably the vast majority of citizens, but the squeaky wheel gets the grease, and the book banners are just that. Our job is to go at this fairly, from both sides, and let our readers decide. As Sergeant Joe Friday used to say, "The facts, ma'am, just the facts.""

"Joe who?" Alison said.

"From the TV series Dragnet, which was big back in the '50s."

"Mort, how do you know all this stuff? You weren't even alive in the '50s."

"My ill-spent youth, I guess," Mort said. "Too much time in front of the TV and not enough with the books."

"Gimme a break," Alison said. "I know your history—valedictorian and Jeopardy champ. Apparently, you had time for other things, as well."

"Ancient history," Mort said. "You're only as good as your current game. And you're right, it was heart-warming to see all those groups and people getting involved to stop book banning. We've got a lot to work with from both perspectives."

They decided that Alison would make the contacts for Oklahoma and Texas, and Mort would take on Arkansas and the state of Florida where Families for Freedom was formed. To his surprise, one of that organization's founders, Meredith Bigote, had readily agreed to an interview.

* * *

Oklahoma was a state that had banned same sex marriage in 2004 until preempted by federal law, a state where a large portion of the population identified as evangelicals. Alison was surprised to find that the state supreme court had rejected an attempt by the state department of education to ban several titles, citing that the books in question were consistent with community standards. However, throughout the state, forty-two books had been removed from school libraries or classrooms by the same department of education, particularly works by Black authors such as Maya Angelou and Frederick Douglass. Harry Potter books were on the banned lists, as well as *To Kill a Mockingbird*, which was consistently found on lists circulated by local groups as well as Families for Freedom.

In Texas, Alison found that the state led the nation in attempting to ban over eight hundred books and ranked first among the states in restricting personal freedoms in school reading choices, including the classic Judy Blume title *Are You There, God? It's Me Margaret*, a multiple award winner which had been made into a motion picture. In one county, a teacher had been removed after reading from an illustrated version of Anne Frank's diary because of a description of female anatomy. Another county had canceled its annual Scholastic Book Fair, its largest fundraiser of the academic year, because of several complaints by right wing citizens.

Mort started his tour in Arkansas before traveling to Florida and his Families for Freedom interview. The Arkansas governor, who denied Mort's request for an interview, had signed into law Act 372 in 2023, which had made it easier to bring prosecutions against librarians or booksellers for distributing books or materials deemed "harmful to minors." Anyone in the state could challenge a publication, even though the terms of the law never fully defined what was harmful. Mort interviewed the editor of the *Arkansas Times*, Bailey Austin, about what was considered "harmful."

"It's in the eye of the beholder," Austin told him, "which is why Democracy Forward, a liberal, nonprofit advocacy group brought a lawsuit in federal district court challenging the law under the First Amendment. *Thank God* for the First Amendment. The judge agreed and enjoined enforcement of several sections of the Act. But that's probably just temporary until they amend the Act."

Mort responded, "These groups don't seem to represent a majority of the people, and these laws place the power of bigotry in the hands of the few. To me, that's not democracy."

"Right on, brother," Austin agreed.

* * *

Florida, like Texas, was the nation's other bastion of book banning. Helped by a right-wing governor and a legislature ready to genuflect, it was only natural, in Mort's opinion, that Florida had spawned Families for Freedom. The organization was very powerful throughout Florida. HB 1069, signed into law by the governor, prohibited any showings of nudity and sexuality to minors. Objectors at a school board meeting questioning the statute were met with derision from the audience.

Threats and hate mail followed. The dog of one of the objectors died mysteriously, although no one could definitively say it was another act of retribution.

In another district, it was ruled illegal for teachers to talk about who they loved or married, and a librarian who talked about her same sex partner was accused of being a pedophile and fired. In a different county, a member of Families for Freedom called the police and filed a complaint over illustrations in a young adult book shelved in a public library because of a minuscule depiction of a penis in an illustration. This was the local Florida atmosphere that Mort entered.

Twenty-four

Mort flew into Orlando, rented a car at the airport, and met Meredith Bigote, one of the founders of Families for Freedom, at the Melbourne branch of the Brevard County Library. He thought it was ironic that they met in a private room in the public library.

Meredith Bigote was an attractive, young-looking blond in her thirties who wore a simple black but decorated blouse, black slacks, flats, and a gold cross on a chain around her neck. As they shook hands, Mort noted that she was almost his height.

"I've read about you," Meredith said. "I'm flattered to be in the company of such a well-known personality."

"Don't be fooled by what you read," Mort said. "I could say the same thing about you. You've got a national following."

"Just people who want to level the moral perspective," Meredith said.

"How did this all get started?"

Meredith launched a well-rehearsed introduction to her story. "Believe it or not, it was the Covid mask mandates and mandatory vaccinations that got it going. Ridiculous to insist on us wearing masks, wasn't it? I was basically a stay-at-home housewife involved in a lot of church and civic organizations. My husband is a pharmacist. We were all basically stuck at home and had a greater chance to see what the schools had our children reading. I have two kids in the district. And some of it was outrageous for kids. Porn, nudity, salacious material that could only warp their minds. So, a group of us talked, Zoomed, got on Facebook and emailed. We found that there were a lot of us who felt our children were in danger. In fact, not only the children, but adults as well. And we had a lot of support from religious leaders as well as legislators. Even one in my family."

"But you've attacked some of the classics—some important historical material like Elie Wiesel's *Night,* various Holocaust books, Pulitzer-prize winners, books that children should be exposed to so that society doesn't repeat some of its worst mistakes."

"You really think that society will learn? Look around at the world today. We've learned nothing. Children don't have to be warped by such horror. And our religious leaders agree. I'm very close to the Catholic Church. Many of my close friends are Evangelical Protestants."

"But you attacked books about race, ethnicity, gender, sexuality, homosexuality, and made it a political agenda," Mort said. "Hiding these things doesn't mean they don't exist, doesn't make them go away."

"But we can keep them out of school curricula, out of school libraries, away from the most impressionable creations—our children," Meredith said.

"The Southern Poverty Law Center has labeled you as a far-right extremist group," Mort pointed out.

"And I label them as left-wing communists," Meredith countered, "the type of organization that is threatening our society. Look, we have opened chapters in every state in just four years, enrolled hundreds of thousands of members. We have organizers in communities all over, a monthly newsletter read by tens of thousands. Doesn't that tell you something? Doesn't that point to a need for our perspective? It started here, yes, but it's now headquartered in the Midwest, in the center of the country. That's where our direction comes from, where the newsletters are published—although all chapters can contribute."

"And inevitably, violence arises out of this rhetoric," Mort said. "I've just been in Jackson, Mississippi, where a young attorney, a mother of two, was killed because she represented a librarian charged in a book banning case."

"Terrible. I read about it. We don't encourage violence. We abhor it," Meredith said. "But some people just get so frustrated about attempts to improve society that they erupt. Unfortunately, people are so intense, so mentally disturbed by the peddling of this filth, especially to children, that they lose it. We certainly don't condone violent acts."

"What about that member of yours in Missouri who was running for secretary of state and used a flame thrower to burn books she deemed objectionable. Showy, but obscene in and of itself, wouldn't you say?"

"We certainly don't condone conduct like that, either. Not an intelligent approach."

"But you didn't condemn it, either," Mort reminded her. "You profess to encourage free thinking. But aren't you *restricting* free thinking by imposing your standards on others? Isn't that what the First Amendment is all about?"

"Mort—may I call you Mort? I can see that you have a different mindset. I suspect that you are a very liberal thinker. Perhaps when you're a parent you'll see our perspective."

"I have twins, not quite two."

"Then there's hope for you," Meredith said, smiling. "And I will certainly pray for you every night, and for your twins."

"I appreciate that," Mort said, "because I need all the help I can get. But I wanted to touch on the religious fervor that your movement has stoked. It seems as though the bulk of your followers, your members, espouse conservative Christian leanings, or am I wrong?"

"No, I would say that for the most part that is the case, but we think of ourselves as a non-partisan organization that is steeped in conservative values. We don't turn anyone away who shares our beliefs no matter who they are. And we encourage spirited dialogue. You must admit, though, that the United States is basically a Christian nation."

"I like to think of it as founded on Judeo-Christian beliefs," Mort said, "much as I believe the Founding Fathers believed."

"Well, so be it," Meredith said. "We don't seek to change anyone's beliefs. But our followers are overwhelmingly supportive."

"You know what the Pied Piper of Hamelin ended up doing to his followers?" Mort asked.

"I don't think I'm familiar with that one."

"Hmm, might be a tale in one of your banned books," Mort said. "But as the legend goes, the town of Hamelin in Germany was overrun with rats, so the mayor hired a man who had a magic pipe or flute to lead the rats into the river to drown. The man played his instrument, and all the rats followed into the river and drowned. And then, once they were gone, the mayor refused to pay him. So, the man got angry, sought revenge, and played his flute again with a different tune until all the children in the town followed him into the river and drowned just as the rats had done. By banning books you are not only damaging the minds of the young, but also depriving them of literature and knowledge that will make them better citizens."

Meredith smiled. "I'm not familiar with that story," she said, "but what we are trying to do is make the world, and our children in particular, better people by keeping them from impurity."

"I guess it's in the eye of the beholder," Mort said. "I appreciate your time and your candor. If you don't mind, I'd like to take a few shots with my phone to go with the story."

They talked a while longer, about some of the incidents of threats and violence that continued to take place around the country, about statistics and events, until Meredith stood and shook Mort's hand.

* * *

Mort flew to Shelter Rock, Kansas, where Alison had already returned. Atticus offered his second bedroom to Danni and Mort. Danni had split off and stayed in Kansas, spending time with Janice Marquand at the library, studying up for her upcoming constitutional law assignment and discussing book banning issues with both Janice and Atticus. She also met briefly with Eric Robbins before taking the obligatory air tour of Kansas with Atticus at the controls of his Cessna.

On the airplane journey back to DC, Danni leaned over toward Mort and said, "Atticus is really an interesting person. I can see how Alison got involved with him so quickly."

"I thought so too," Mort said. "She deserves it. She's had a rocky dating career from what I know."

"Another thing," Danni said. "As long as she's involved with Atticus, I don't have to worry about you ending up in her bed again."

"You don't quit, even in jest," Mort said. "Not to worry, when you have steak—"

"Don't say it!" Danni admonished.

Twenty-five

Alison's story on the *Clarion* raid and related issues had been given a front page, lead-in column in the *Post*, and then full-page coverage inside the paper. Even though the story was almost a month old, the in-depth coverage, including thoughtful interviews and Alison's insights, got attention from media and newspapers around the nation.

Alison was flushed with excitement when she told Mort, "I can't believe this. I just heard from Senator Wellton's office, and they want me to come up to the capitol for a conference with her and several other senators about press freedoms. Bipartisan, they said. Can you believe that?"

"Bipartisan?" Mort said. "There's practically nothing in Washington that's bipartisan anymore. It was a great article, Alison, but it must have really struck some raw nerves. Maybe there's hope for the Constitution, after all."

They talked briefly, and Mort suggested that the first step would be to report to Marcie before proceeding. "This is a real feather in your cap," Mort said.

Marcie Gold was equally excited about Alison's invitation and urged her to accept immediately.

"Do I need an attorney to go with me?" Alison asked.

Marcie laughed. "You're not testifying in a senate hearing," she said. "They apparently just want to meet with you and pick your brain. None of the articles anywhere in the country had the insight and the depth of your material. I heard a rumor within the last few weeks that several senators are considering a bill to shield the press from the kind of conduct that paper in Kansas endured. Apparently, rage has filtered all the way up the ladder."

***

A week later, Alison was nervously seated in a large conference room with a flotilla of government officials in the Russell Senate Office Building. There were eventually three senators, with numerous staff members. Senator Wellton, who was from Wisconsin, warmly shook Alison's hand when she entered. She was a buxom, sixtyish woman several inches shorter than Alison. Wellton had a distinctive look with rouged cheeks, bright red lipstick and nails.

Following Senator Wellton into the room was a short, balding man in shirtsleeves Alison recognized as Senator Klee from Utah. A few minutes later, Senator Duncan from Michigan entered. His wiry, six-foot-five frame gave him the look of a basketball player compared to the others in the room.

Two democrats and a republican, Alison thought. Truly bipartisan. The assemblage complimented Alison on her article, which Senator Wellton described ironically as a phony "search and seizure." They wanted to know more about the people behind the conduct in Shelter Rock and what led up to the now infamous event.

"Well," Alison said, "there had been a lot of animosity building up for a long period because Mrs. Robbins of the Clarion was known for fearlessly digging deep and ruffling feathers—even into her nineties."

"But did she do anything illegal or unethical?" Senator Duncan asked in a deep baritone.

"Oh, no," Alison said. "She was just a lady who questioned government when it appeared to have strayed from the straight and narrow. And she was inevitably correct, my reporting showed. I believe that it was the stress of the raid that killed her."

The senators all expressed their regret for her death and the conduct that preceded it. They questioned Alison for about a half hour, thanked her for her input and left. On the way out, Senator Wellton said to one of her staff, "Ralph, make certain that we have all of Alison's contact information."

* * *

Three weeks later, the senators introduced the Margery Robbins Federal Press Act. Among its provisions, it barred law enforcement from unduly harassing journalists and protected their sources, emails and records. It also made it much more difficult to get search warrants of journalists unless national security was involved, or evidence of a criminal activity was evident.

Alison was speechless when a courier delivered a copy of the proposed bill to her desk with a note of thanks from Senator Wellton.

Eric Robbins was practically in tears when he called Alison after news of the proposed bill was formally introduced. "It would have meant so much to Mom," he said.

* * *

Alison and Atticus were talking on their phones nightly, and he was effervescent about her new-found fame. His ardor was even increased when, two weeks after Alison's article about the *Clarion*, the book banning article she co-authored with Mort, became a three-day feature in the *Post* and got national attention.

"I guess now you're too famous for a poor school teacher from Kansas," Atticus said.

"Try me," Alison said.

"That's what I've been attempting to do since we met," Atticus said. "You know that article about book banning and Families for Freedom accomplished something that nothing else has done."

"What's that?"

"It drove my ex bonkers. She even called me and ranted. Cursed, even, which she rarely does because she's 'born again.' About you, I might add. Said you attacked her integrity and everyone in that organization, or cult, or whatever. She said all they were trying to do is protect children and restore Christianity to its proper place in society."

"What did you say?"

"Well, honestly, I kind of lost it," Atticus said. "I reminded her that when I wanted us to raise a family, she was too busy or too involved to even consider it. Thank God, in retrospect. Now, it looks like she's apparently become even more ultrareligious. Spends hours each day with Father Hoffmann at the church."

"Really? She must have a lot to confess. Or is there *another* reason?"

Atticus didn't want to talk about his ex anymore, so they changed the subject and tried to figure out when and how often they could get together. They decided that Atticus would come to Washington in a week, and a week later Alison would fly to Kansas to see him and also Eric Robbins at the *Clarion*.

Twenty-six

The three-day series on book banning was carried nationally by all the papers that licensed *Washington Post* syndicated content. Other papers, which did not regularly reprint *Post* content, made arrangements to do so. Many of them, because of the growing interest in book banning, republished the articles over three days as the *Post* had done.

The series, or snippets and synopses of it, found its way into magazines like *Time* and *Newsweek* and professional periodicals by *PEN America* and *The Author's Guild*. It also became a subject of editorials in daily newspapers like the *New York Times, Boston Globe* and the *Chicago Tribune*. Mort received over two dozen offers to appear on national TV or at forums and academic seminars, while Alison received about half as many. They assumed that his prior notoriety and *Pulitzer* credentials were the reason for his greater number of invitations. In several cases, they were invited to appear together.

Alison was at her desk when she saw an email from Eric Robbins of the *Clarion*. He asked permission to reprint the series in its entirety, once a week over three weeks in the *Clarion*. His email read: "You know that we operate on a shoestring, so that if we could get permission to reprint without having to pay for it, it would relieve a burden for us." The request passed from Alison to Mort to Marcie Gold, who readily gave her official permission.

But accolades were not the only thing the reporters received. Mort got dozens of derogatory emails criticizing the articles and their imagined intrusion into people's beliefs. Inevitably, some came with intimidating language and threats. One angry soul wrote, "You are one of the Godless, attempting to pervert our children, and you will be punished for your sins." Another wrote, "You probably feast on the blood of children." The most succinct ones simply wrote "Fuck you," or "I hope you die a horrible death."

Alison was not prepared for attacks on her anatomy and imagined moral indiscretions. She began screening her emails and phone calls. One afternoon, she received a package at her desk with a white powder that was immediately turned over to security, who brought in the DC police. Analysis showed that it was just talcum powder, but the message was clear and threatening. The sender, as usual, was anonymous.

"They're the ones who don't have the cajónes to identify themselves," Mort told Alison. "They're basically cowards who don't have the courage or intellect to confront you, so they do it by intimidation. It's no different from what so many librarians and school board members have experienced—and still endure."

"That may be true," Alison said, "but it's unnerving."

"Look at what these same morons did to poll workers and election volunteers after the 2020 elections," Mort reminded her. "Election volunteers, for Christ's sake—volunteers who give up their time and part of their lives to make certain our elections are conducted fairly and freely."

"I know you're right," Alison said, "but it still freaks me out. A librarian in Idaho was just attacked by a man who asked for assistance and then tried to punch her in the head. When she sought help, he began yelling slurs at her. Even threatened her life."

"We know these things happen," Mort said. "For the most part, though, these threats are not carried out. It's the ones that are, of course, that create fear in all the targets."

* * *

It was later that afternoon when Mort's cell phone told him it was Danni calling. Danni, who was normally calm and grounded, was practically hysterical. "Someone was at our place when I was at my law school office. Juanita was with the kids. They rang the bell and she went to the door, checked the security camera and didn't see anyone. But when she opened the door she found a bloody, dead chicken on the step with a note that said, 'We know where you live. It would be terrible if anything happened to those twins.' Mort, I'm frightened."

Being frightened were words that Mort had never heard from Danni.

"Holy shit!" Mort exclaimed. "Did you call the cops?"

"Of course, that's the first thing I did. They're on their way. But the kids—I'm really freaked out, and Juanita is out of her mind."

"I'll be there as soon as I can. Keep the door locked and don't do anything."

"Thanks," Danni said with a twinge of sarcasm. "I wouldn't have figured that out by myself. This is way out of hand, Mort. These people are crazy."

Mort told Alison why he was leaving so suddenly.

Alison said, "My God! That's terrible. But to quote you only an hour ago, 'We know these things happen. But for the most part they're not carried out and are only to create fear.'"

"A bloody chicken on our doorstep. And threats to my kids! I'd like to kill that son of a bitch. This is more than a threat. It's physical intimidation."

On the short drive home, Mort decided on a plan of action. He would move Danni and the kids to Travilah immediately to be with J.J. and Chickie, and then he'd commute back and forth to the paper. It was only twenty miles. Danni had most of her time free over the summer until fall semester, which would give the police time to conduct a full investigation. He would get on the horn with Supreme Court Police Chief and close friend Travis Anderson, as well as notify his friend in the FBI, Special Agent Craig Fisher, who would follow up. After all, he thought, the twins are the grandchildren of a supreme court justice, and there are federal statutes in the US Code that make such threats federal felonies.

Mort thought back to Danni's stalker who had come with a pistol into their living room two years earlier. Danni, who hated guns, had fired Mort's pistol, which he had insisted she learn how to use, at the intruder, and that man was now in a mental institution. Or was he? Mort would have to check that out.

Twenty-seven

The exodus to Travilah took place in two cars. Danni transported the twins in her Subaru, and Mort followed in his SUV with Katie plus all the clothing and other essentials his family would require.

The following day, Mort got a message from Danni while seated at his desk. "We got a call on the answering machine at home from a detective, Sergeant Don Donaldson. He asked us to give a call for an update and left his number. I'll let you call him since you have a regular relationship with the police."

Mort said, "Thanks a lot," wrote down the number and called the detective.

Donaldson said, "Mr. Ahrens, I have some information I think you'll find very interesting. Are you going to be at home later this afternoon or this evening?"

They made an appointment to meet at his home late in the afternoon. Mort had planned to drive to Travilah directly from the office, but this information took precedence.

After Mort arrived at the Georgetown condo, he sorted the mail. To his surprise, one of the items was a Families for Freedom newsletter and a welcome letter thanking "Katie Springer" for joining. He had forgotten they had enrolled their dog online several days earlier.

Thumbing through the newsletter, he was even more surprised to see that Tish Duvall, Atticus's ex, was the editor. The masthead indicated that the publication was headquartered in Shelter Rock,

Kansas. He recalled that Meredith Bigote said that operations had moved to the Midwest.

Detective Sergeant Donaldson arrived promptly, introduced himself, and they moved into the living room. Donaldson was a tall Black man in a sports coat with closely cropped hair that made him look almost bald. "I think you're going to be surprised at our findings," he said.

"I'm not sure that I need any more surprises," Mort said. "But surprise me anyway."

"First, forensics found a partial fingerprint on the note left with the dead chicken. Sloppy job by the perp. They were able to get a match."

"Easier than I imagined," Mort said. "And the winner is…?"

"Not what you expected, I think," Donaldson said. "I know from your complaint that you thought it had something to do with your newspaper articles."

"And?"

"And you'll recall those two young men that you surprised in that attempted carjacking? Well, the one you knocked over the railing was Otis Campanaro, who had a pretty full rap sheet for a twenty-year-old. It was his prints on the note."

"I'll be damned!" Mort said. "I didn't see that coming. But how come he was out on the street and not in jail? And how did he get all the information about us—the address, the twins? That's pretty scary."

"There are no more secrets in this world," Donaldson said. "Anyone with a little ingenuity can dig it all out, especially on someone like you, so well-known. He was probably really pissed because you broke his arm and decided to get some revenge. Don't worry, though. We just picked him up, and now he's charged with terrorist threats among other things. Last time, he got out on bail and was still out when he pulled this stunt. This time he'll be away for a long time. He'll be arraigned tomorrow. The sad part of the story is his mother."

"What's with her?" Mort asked.

"Kim Campanaro is a single mother working two jobs and raising three kids. The other two are apparently good kids. She put up her house as collateral for her son's bail on the carjacking, and now she's probably going to lose the house. He isn't worth a devoted woman like that."

"How much was the bail?"

"She came up with seven thousand by pledging the house. Now that he's been busted again, unless she can come up with the cash, she loses the homestead," Donaldson said.

"Shit," Mort said. "Why is it that the innocent are always the ones to suffer? Will she really lose her house?"

"Unfortunately, yes. She just doesn't have the money."

"Not gonna happen," Mort said. "Can you get me the information on the bond?"

"What you got in mind?" Donaldson asked.

"Simple. I'll give this guy his seven grand, and that'll square things."

"You'd do that for someone you never met?" Donaldson seemed dumbfounded.

"Look, I'm partly responsible," Mort said. "My martial arts training enabled me to kick that rotten kid over the railing. His mother shouldn't have to suffer. Certainly not at the cost of her house. The bondsman will get his money, and she gets to keep what she's worked for."

"You are a most unusual man," Donaldson said. "I'll get you that information, but first, will you do me a favor?"

"What's that?"

"Let me shake your hand."

"And you can do me a favor too," Mort said.

"Which is?"

"Let's keep this between us and the bail bondsman. I don't need any more publicity."

Donaldson said he'd get back to Mort right away and keep his end of the bargain. "You know the word *mensch*?" he asked.

"Those are my people," Mort said, smiling.

Donaldson shook his hand vigorously and left.

The bail bondsman, however, was not part of the agreement, and Mort was mortified a few days later when a story appeared in the

Washington Times about the hero reporter who paid the bondsman to save the home of an attacker's mother.

When he arrived at his desk the day after the story broke, there was a golden halo on his desk with the legend "Saint Mort."

Twenty-eight

Mort was at his desk looking over the day's *Post* when he suddenly exclaimed, "Holy shit!" Danni and the twins were still in Travilah. Mort had made an early morning commute. He whipped his feet off the desk and immediately sat up straight as he pulled the paper closer.

The story that startled him was an article on the Opinion page entitled "Counterpoint." It was in response to his and Alison's three articles on book banning. The authors were Meredith Bigote and Tish Duvall, ex-wife of Atticus. Under his breath, he said, "Son of a bitch!" He read the column again more slowly, more carefully. In part, it read:

> While the *Post* undoubtedly expended a large amount of money to send their reporters all over the Southern states, their lack of objectivity was patently obvious. From the outset, it is clear that they had determined to portray Families for Freedom as a right-wing and irresponsible organization, consistent with others of similar beliefs, whose emphasis is political rather than ecumenical. Nothing could be further from the truth.
>
> It is true that Families for Freedom closely adheres to the principles of Christianity, but we make no apology for that. It is the departure from Christian beliefs that has thrown this nation into chaos. Violence is rampant, and Godliness has become secondary to the beliefs of not only our political leaders, but obviously to what was once a respected organ of the press, *The Washington Post*.

What our nucleus and ideology believe in is the rule of law with peaceful and meaningful discourse; we fail to understand why a Godless minority would object to it when the focus is on what is good and wholesome in society, especially for our children and those unable to defend themselves. We are proud to endorse the Ten Commandments, the rule of law, and the scriptures. We detest the fact that we have to monitor our schools, public bodies and organizations such as libraries to prevent our children from having access to books and materials that are obscene, pornographic, inappropriate, and unquestionably damaging to their psyches. This filth should not be disseminated or available to the unwary and vulnerable. If, in our mission, we have to endure the slings and arrows of the unworthy, so be it, but we would expect more from institutions such as the *Washington Post*. Dialogue is one thing, one-sided and bigoted dissemination of those who would usurp the dictates of the Almighty is unacceptable.

While the First Amendment protects freedom and speech, it does not permit unbridled access to harmful and detrimental materials. It is axiomatic that you cannot yell "Fire!" in a crowded theater; it is no less important to protect us from conduct that is equally dangerous.

The article was co-authored by Meredith Bigote, the Florida mother Mort had just interviewed in Florida, and Tish Duvall, editor of the Families for Freedom newsletter, the *Liberty National*. Tish Duvall was the Evangelical ex-wife of Atticus. Mort headed straight for Marcie's office.

"I was wondering how long it would take you to get here," Marcie said.

"Our article was factual," Mort insisted. "We didn't editorialize, we didn't take sides, and all we did was relate what's in the public record, dammit."

"I know that, you know that, but these people have become a force to reckon with and a political power as well, so we have to take criticism as it comes, but with the proverbial grain of salt," Marcie said. "I've already heard from our new editor-in-chief who suggested that you might write a sort of 'clarification' letter explaining what you just told me."

"Mortensen? The Brit who came from Fox News? Now there's an oxymoron for you, Fox and news in the same sentence. Mortenson is a man who was accused of God-knows-what ethical violations years ago in the UK—a case that is now apparently being revived. Deleting thousands of emails, right? And he wants a 'clarification' letter! No way! He can have my job first."

"I already expressed those same sentiments," Marcie said. "I'm meeting with him in an hour. He's also got some other crazy ideas about reorganizing things around here that I will not abide."

"How the hell did he ever become the editor-in-chief of the Post, anyway?"

"The owner gets to pick who he wants," Marcie said. "But I think he had some surprises with this guy. Probably shock. He obviously wasn't vetted very well."

* * *

A little over an hour later, Alison was trying to soothe Mort's anger as she sat in his cubicle.

"People get to say whatever they want in Counterpoints as long as their remarks are not obscene," Alison said.

"But they mischaracterized our article," Mort said. "That's what pisses me off."

They looked up as Marcie appeared suddenly. "Meeting in the conference room in an hour," she said. "For everyone in the unit."

After they assembled, almost sixty reporters were crammed into a space designed for about twenty.

"I'm not going to sugar-coat this," Marcie said, looking somber. "I just resigned, effective immediately, and I wanted you all to know before anyone else. All of your jobs are secure. I have been assured of that, and now I have to clean out my office. Good luck."

There was a stunned silence. "Wait," Mort said. "Don't leave us hanging like this. What the hell is going on?"

"Let's just say that the new editor-in-chief and I have very different ideas on how to run a newspaper," Marcie said before she walked out.

A memo circulated that afternoon under the byline of Cecil Mortensen, Editor-in-Chief. It started by thanking Marcie Gold for her service to the *Post* and for her years in journalism and then stated that until a new managing editor was chosen, reporters and section chiefs would report directly to him.

Within an hour, a letter written by Mort and signed by all the reporters who worked for Marcie, was forwarded to the owner, objecting to what had just transpired:

> We, the undersigned, all employees of the *Post* and working under the aegis of Managing Editor Marcie Gold, register our objection to the treatment that necessitated her resigning her position. Some of us are considering similar resignations. Marcie, an incredible journalist and leader, was in many respects responsible not only for Pulitzer Prizes and other awards, but for fostering an atmosphere of congeniality and competence in the pressroom. Our new editor-in-chief, an individual of questionable background and clearly not familiar with our high standards, left her no choice but to resign because of his arrogant and high-handed tactics. We urge you to review this matter and facilitate her return.

Twenty-nine

Ten days later, as he sat across from Dr. Silverstein in his martial arts outfit, Mort answered Silverstein's question about whether his threat to resign was real or just a bluff.

"It was an honest threat," Mort said. "That clown, Mortenson, would have ruined what Steve Ginsberg started and Marcie continued so effectively. It was a terrific atmosphere to work in. Looking forward to your job is a big incentive."

"But what about salary and stability for the family?" Silverstein said.

"Of course I discussed it with Danni, and she encouraged me," Mort said. "She wants me to be happy in my work. Fortunately, we're in a position where we could manage financially. And if I had resigned, I would have gone to one of the search firms and landed something very quickly with the credentials I have. Or, if necessary, Steve would have taken me in New York."

"Those are the same credentials that you regularly underestimate, if I'm not mistaken," Silverstein said.

Mort smiled and said, "They apparently surface when needed."

"Why can't that same confidence be there all the time?"

"Apparently, I need something to trigger me, to get the blood flowing."

"You had no doubt about your hazardous decision?" Silverstein said.

"None whatsoever," Mort said. "It was the right thing to do, and I did it."

"You were the organizer of the uprising, so to speak?"

"Looking back," Mort said, "I guess so. Everyone was really pissed. I just was the loudest."

"So, to put this in context, you took the lead and were successful. How does that square with your feelings of inadequacy?"

"I'll have to think about that one," Mort said. "Maybe I'm moving forward. Bottom line, the Brit is out and Marcie is negotiating her return. Hopefully, business as usual."

"With you," Silverstein said, "it's rarely business as usual. The usual is winning awards, solving murders, getting involved where others would hesitate, and performing unexpected acts—like posting your own funds to save the house of a woman you've never met and whose son is an attacker who might have killed you. And then undervaluing yourself." With that, Silverstein looked at the wall clock and said, "To be continued."

* * *

That evening in Travilah, Mort told Danni, "Irwin seems to think that I require something to trigger me to act in these odd situations I often find myself in. Probably to overcome a lack of self-confidence."

"Irwin?" Danni said. "You're now on a first name basis?"

"Not to his face," Mort said, "but he's helped me a lot, I think. What do you think?"

"I think that you love getting into these difficult situations to challenge yourself. Then, when you're successful, you don't believe in yourself enough to recognize you are a natural leader."

"Jesus!" Mort said. "That might be the nicest thing you ever said to me."

"Don't let it go to your head."

"I can't, because I'm still working on my self-confidence, remember?"

They decided it was time to return to Georgetown with the twins. There had been no further threats in two weeks, and what they had initially thought was a threat from Families for Freedom turned out to have nothing to do with the book banning series. Once

Marcie was back at the *Post,* they would finally get to go on that long-delayed vacation.

Danni thought a river cruise somewhere in Europe would be perfect, but that uninterrupted week away was still a dream, and a lot could happen before then. She had heard good reports about Viking cruises from some of her associates at the law school.

* * *

Back in Georgetown, and bedding the twins for the night, Mort was going through the mail and found the monthly Families for Freedom newsletter sent to new member Katie Springer. Since Katie had been fed and walked, she was more interested in napping than reading the newsletter, so Mort decided to see what it contained.

"Wow," he said to Danni. "The feature article for the month is from Father Hoffmann, the priest in Shelter Rock. The church seems to be really getting involved in the political side of things and supporting book banning full throttle."

"He say anything of interest?" Danni asked.

"Well, the usual prattle about our duty to protect children and the vulnerable from material that 'they' deem objectionable, but what surprises me is how he readily involved the Church in all this. I wonder if the diocese is aware that he's trampling on that fragile line between church and state?"

"I think that line has already been obliterated," Danni said, then went back to checking her emails. A few moments later, she exclaimed, "My God. Theo Bickel died unexpectedly yesterday, and the dean wants to see me tomorrow."

"Bickel?"

"Our Con Ed professor at the law school. I don't think you ever met him. The reclusive type. Not only had worldwide respect, but he had an endowed chair. Apparently, it was a heart attack."

"How old was he, and how does that affect you?"

"I guess we'll find out tomorrow," Danni said. "He was in his early sixties. I don't know that it affects me at all since I teach environmental law."

"But you clerked for a great constitutional scholar—J.J. Maybe they want you to inquire if he'd be interested in the job. You are his stepdaughter, after all. Plus, J.J. is in his eighties, and there's been talk of his retiring for years."

"You know J.J. won't retire while there is still a conservative majority on the court," Danni said. "He sees himself as a beacon of light in the darkness. But maybe that's what the dean wanted. We'll find out soon enough."

Thirty

⤐◦◦◦◦⤏

Shelter Rock, Kansas

On the same Saturday that Mort and Danni returned home, Alison was back in Kansas. She and Atticus were alternating visits with two weeks in between each trip. So far, it was working.

Alison had visited with Eric Robbins at the *Clarion* earlier in the day and shared that visit with Atticus over lunch at C.B. Baked Goods. "Eric didn't seem like himself," she said. "He has slowed down and looks very pale. He's lost a lot of hair in a short time."

"He hasn't been well," Atticus said, "which is why I've been spending a lot of time with him at the paper to see what I can do to help. He said he's been vomiting, has terrible diarrhea and feels like he's not nearly as sharp as usual. They did some tests, but nothing turned up. Must be some kind of a bug he has to work out of his system."

"What can you do around the paper? You writing anything?"

"No, that's your department. I'm like a volunteer go-fer, and I pick up a lot of gossip from drop-ins and the ladies in the front."

"Gossip? Such as…?"

"Such as my ex has been spending an incredible amount of time with the priest at the church."

"You said she was practically born again. And she's active in Families for Freedom, right?"

"It's more than just that. Day and night—or at least into the evenings, from what I hear. Sounds like they've got something cooking. He's a real right-wing reactionary, too, the clergy or not. Like a warrior priest. Just like so many of the alleged Christian conservative evangelicals. But Father Hoffmann seems to be fond of Eric for some bizarre reason. Stops in at the paper every couple of days. Even brings him donuts. I think they come from the mayor, from what Eric says. I'm talking too much, aren't I?"

"You kidding? Tell me more."

Atticus shrugged and spoke again. "The mayor hates the Clarion, which has been blasting him for years, but the city is scared shitless that Eric hasn't started a lawsuit about the search and the Donnelly woman whose hand was broken when they yanked her cell phone away. It's just weird. Especially since Eric's written several more terrific editorials about the scourge of book banning. And he's been really harsh about the mayor and the council and their fast and loose form of governing. Just like his mother was."

"Look," Alison said, "maybe the priest is just doing his job and being ecumenical after Margery's death. And your ex, maybe you just dislike her so much that you're suspicious of anything she's involved in. My advice? Move on, fellow. Get a life. I thought that's what I'm for."

"You're right. And I love you for it."

* * *

Back in DC on Monday morning, Alison had returned and reported on her weekend visit with Atticus and Eric Robbins and was still sitting in Mort's office. Until Marcie returned, Mort had been designated to attend the editorial meetings, but their assignments had been mundane for the most part with a lot of positive feedback still coming in from the book banning series.

Mort picked up his phone when he saw it was from Danni. "What's up?" he asked.

"You'll never guess what the dean wanted," Danni said.

"He wants you to take over the constitutional law class."

"How the hell did you know…?"

"He checked with me first to get my permission."

"Bullshit!"

"Okay, bullshit. But truthfully, I figured they'd be looking for someone who can get up to speed quickly, and they couldn't find a better candidate than you. Especially because of your background with the Supremes, Baby Love." Mort started humming the biggest hit of the Supremes.

"Mort, be serious. This is a big deal, not a '70s singing group. But there's more…" Danni said, pausing without finishing her sentence.

"Which is…? I'm waiting."

Alison got up and moved to the hall, signaling with her hands and mouthing, "Later."

Mort waved her off.

Danni continued. "Which is… a promotion to associate professor from assistant professor. But there's a downside."

"No more money?" Mort said.

"Morton. Be serious." She only called him "Morton" when she was getting exasperated.

"No, it probably means another seven to ten grand," Danni said. "But it means I'll have to work like crazy for the rest of the summer to get ready for the semester. So, once again, there goes our vacation. I told him I'd let him know after I spoke with you."

"Honey," Mort said, and then wondered how that term of endearment, which he didn't recall having ever used before, had come out of his mouth. "I am so proud of you. Associate professor in such a short time. And at your age. Anyway, that vacation seems to be eluding us, but good things happen every time it does. You must take the job, of course, and that even leaves a big opportunity for me."

"Opportunity? I don't understand," Danni said.

"I can give up my job, become a stay-at-home dad with the twins and write that novel I've always wanted to take a shot at."

"Morton!" Danni exploded.

"Okay, okay," Mort said. "I'll keep my job. But this is a no-brainer. I'm so proud of you. Associate professor. I can't wait to tell the folks."

"Don't hang up," Danni said. "There's more."

"What more could there be?" Mort asked.

"The law school was asked by Fox News to have Professor Bickel do an interview on the First Amendment with Sean Slattery—basically focusing on book banning and constitutional considerations. And that interview is slated for two weeks from now."

"Fox News?"

"Yes, I know… I suggested that you would be a better choice, based on your recent series, but the dean was very specific that they wanted an academic."

"Look, no doubt that you can do it. You're certainly conversant, you know the law. You've been right on top of things as I've prepared the series, and you're much prettier than Sean Slattery."

"Mort!"

"I'm serious. You were great in that televised debate a couple of years ago on the water shortage. You won going away. And this is only an interview. Probably ten minutes. You can do it."

"I wish I had your confidence. I'll talk to the dean again and see what comes out of it. And I'll say yes to the teaching offer, but I'll have to bust my back to get ready for the semester."

"Which will only help you to prepare for the interview," Mort said. "So, it's a no-brainer. Do you want me to call the folks with the good news?"

"No, I'll call Mom and J.J. right now. Much to do. Very exciting. I'll see you at home tonight, but I might be late."

"No worries," Mort said. "I'll call Juanita right now and tell her not to prepare dinner. I'll bring home something special for us to celebrate."

Thirty-one

Melbourne, Florida

Meredith Bigote opened the front door of her ranch home, smiled and warmly embraced the tall man who stood on the top step. The house on a cul-de-sac was set back from the street by about sixty feet. A driveway led up to a connected two-car garage on the west side, partly hidden by extensive plantings and foliage on a two-acre plot.

"Oh, Ed," Meredith said. "I'm so glad you could come. I've needed to talk to you so desperately, but it had to be in person, not over the phone or on Zoom."

"You sounded panicked," Ed said, "so I dropped everything and hopped the first plane I could get. What's the problem? Larry? The kids? Tell me."

"Larry doesn't even know that I called you," Meredith said, "and the children are at day camp. But they'll all be thrilled to see you. It's really involved. I needed your advice and counsel. And then you can hear my confession. I wouldn't trust anyone else. How long can you stay?"

"Well, I'd like to be home in time for services on Saturday evening, but the diocese knows I'm here, for a family emergency, so the deacon can conduct if I'm not back in time."

Meredith said, "Come in, come in, you must be starved. Airline food leaves much to be desired."

"As a matter of fact, I didn't eat, not even at the layover, so food and a cup of coffee would be great."

Ed was Father Edvard Hoffmann, the priest of Saint John's Nepomucene Catholic Church in Shelter Rock, Kansas. He was the older brother of Meredith Bigote. His red hair was combed close to his head, and he was dressed in a light-gray business suit with an open-necked shirt. He towered over his sister as she led him to the kitchen.

Father Hoffmann had long been distraught about the freedoms that permeated literature and the publishing industry. They were antagonistic not only to his personal beliefs, but to the teachings of the Church. Children and the vulnerable should not be subjected to what was available in books, in media, or through social media, which seemed to have placed a cell phone in the hands of every child over six years of age. Society should step forward to control this abomination, he felt, which was damaging the moral values and the minds of millions. What was needed was some sort of control.

Father Hoffmann was outspoken from the pulpit and in his occasional published articles, but he sought an opportunity to expand his beliefs on a greater scale. He saw a vehicle to do that in his sister, Meredith (Hoffmann) Bigote, a devoted Catholic and conservative, a mother, an active and respected member of the community, and a resident of Florida, a state led by a conservative governor and legislature.

The COVID-19 pandemic afforded him that opportunity. People were isolated in their homes, there was confusion on both a governmental, medical, and local level on how to confront the disease, and statistics of death and serious illnesses were skyrocketing. One line of thinking was that everyone should get vaccinated with a new vaccine created in an amazingly short time, while others felt that the vaccine was dangerous and had disastrous side effects. Some officials went so far as to recommend injecting bleach to stem the disease. Others felt that people should just "wait it out, it's like the flu."

The time to strike, Father Hoffmann reasoned, was now, when people were both frightened and confused. Fear was a great motivator of such an uneasy populace.

He had called his sister early in the pandemic and suggested a solution to what he saw as a society run amok. They had previously discussed what they both saw as a danger to society in unfettered availability of any sort of literature. Why not get together with a group of friends and neighbors of equal persuasion and start forming book clubs to review some of the dangerous literature available to children in public libraries, and even more frightening, in schools. Meredith relished the idea, especially as a mother of two young children who had a husband with a similar mindset.

"Why can't you do that right in Kansas?" Meredith had asked. "Where you're known, and you have contact with so many people. Your influence could go a long way."

"Two reasons," Edvard had replied. "One, even though my opinions are well-known and public, it might be construed as an official position by the Church, which would not be a good thing. And two, in Kansas we have that liberal Governor Kelly. Even abortion is legal there. They overwhelmingly rejected a referendum to make it illegal. I don't think the pushback about initiating the book banning in Kansas would be wise. Good Heavens! No, Kansas would not be a good move. But Florida, led by a citizen group, would be ideal."

Meredith saw the logic behind her older brother's reasoning. After numerous calls back and forth, Families for Freedom was born. Neither brother nor sister could have anticipated, however, how the organization would mushroom into a national powerhouse in just a few years.

Within a short time, people from around the nation were calling Meredith for information, wanting to form chapters of the organization and become involved. It became more than she and her friends could handle, so they became the titular heads and moved the headquarters of the organization quietly to Shelter Rock, Kansas, where Father Hoffmann headed a small congregation in a tiny community.

Families for Freedom soon attracted the attention of conservative political groups, and suddenly funding was abundant. Father Hoffmann recruited his close friend, parishioner, and fellow believer, Tish Duvall, to become active and create a newsletter. Soon, they were mailing and emailing monthly information nationwide. He and Tish began spending an inordinate amount of time together.

* * *

They were seated in an alcove with windows looking out over a peaceful inlet. Father Hoffmann had a cup of coffee in front of him and was munching on some cookies. "So, what was so serious that you needed to speak to me personally like this?" he asked.

"We…" Meredith said, "meaning Larry and I, have gotten ourselves into a situation which can be threatening, embarrassing, humiliating… It promises to do irreparable damage to everything we've been working for."

"Everything, meaning…?"

"Families for Freedom, our standing in the community—everything," Meredith said. She twisted a napkin in her hands until it shredded. "When we started all this, I first started talking about the possibilities with my best friend, Chelsea McGowan, and then Chelsea and I became the faces of Families for Freedom, as you know. Two well-known mothers gave the organization a certain imprimatur. Chelsea also has two children, and she's divorced. She rotates custody with her ex-husband a week at a time. He bought a house only two blocks from her.

"Anyway, we started spending a lot of time together. Chelsea would even stay over at my place many nights when we were working late. Then, after a while, things started getting, you know, involved."

"Involved? How?" Father Hoffmann asked.

"Involved. Sexually involved. Chelsea is a very attractive woman, and suddenly she was in our bed. With Larry and me. Things kind of got out of hand."

"You mean the three of you were having sex together?"

Meredith nodded and said, "I know it's a sin. But Larry was involved, too, and Chelsea is sexual, and things just evolved. Don't get me wrong. I love her and so does Larry, but…"

"But?"

"Her ex-husband found out and was hysterical. Said he was going to go public with it. He couldn't care less about Families for Freedom. Said he didn't want his children to be brought up in that sort of an atmosphere."

"My God, the children were not involved, were they?" Father Hoffmann asked, astonished.

"Of course not," Meredith said. "But Brittany was having a nightmare one night and walked in and found the three of us, uh, how do you say it? In the act?"

Father Hoffmann sighed deeply. "Not good. Not good at all. But how did the ex-husband find out?"

"The kids are all friends," Meredith said, "and, well, kids talk, and Brittany said something to their daughter—her friend—and it got back to Chelsea's ex. Of course, we broke it off, but now he wants full custody with her only having visitation rights, and he says he's going public unless she agrees."

"You have created quite a problem," Father Hoffmann said.

"I know. And I know I've sinned—the three of us—but I couldn't even go to confession with Father O'Donlin, our priest, because he knows us all so well. I just couldn't face him."

"You know that the confession is sacred, and that your priest could never disclose any of this," Father Hoffmann said.

"Of course, but it was just too embarrassing for him to know about us."

"Meredith, we are all sinners. We have all transgressed. But let's sit down and figure out where we go from here."

Thirty-two

At dinner that evening, after the children were excused, Meredith and her brother and husband, Larry, were having coffee in the large dining room. The men were smoking cigars.

"Meredith explained the problem to me," Father Hoffmann said, "and I'm not certain that there's anything specific that I can do. Of course, I can take your confession, Larry, as I already did with my sister."

"Frankly," Larry Bigote said, "religion was never all that big a thing with me, as you know. I just accommodate Meredith, basically."

"Nonetheless, the offer stands," Father Hoffmann said.

Meredith stood up and said, "I don't know how you two can smoke those things." She gathered up the cups and dessert plates and went into the kitchen.

"I wanted to thank you for that package, by the way," Father Hoffmann said to Larry. "How are things at the drug store?"

"Business has been good since COVID," Larry said. "Was that what your friend needed?"

"Not my friend," Father Hoffmann said, "but a parishioner. Something about experimenting with some sort of myocardial imaging. He's a pseudoscientist. But it was just what was needed, apparently. Just not easy to come by in the middle of Kansas."

* * *

Father Hoffmann left on Saturday morning, drove back to Orlando in the car he had rented, and was back in Shelter Rock in time to conduct the Saturday evening service.

Chelsea refused to give up partial custody. Her husband, as promised, went public with his allegations. It was the kind of story that the papers feast upon, and it ended up going nationwide. As a result, the other directors on the board of Families for Freedom, as well as their conservative political benefactors, felt it would be best if both Meredith and Chelsea resigned, which they did.

* * *

Georgetown, District of Columbia

Danni and Mort were sitting up in bed, she in a Syracuse Orange T-shirt and he in a pair of shorts. Danni had several books spread out around her. Mort got out of the bed and started practicing some of his Krav Maga moves while watching the evening news.

She glanced over at him and smiled. "Go to it, killer," she taunted.

Mort was distracted by the newscast, however. "Jesus," he said, gesturing to the screen. "That's the woman I just interviewed in Florida. The founder of Families for Freedom. She co-authored that vehement critique of our article."

"And is she on the news as a result of your powerful interview?" Danni asked with a smirk.

"Not quite," Mort said. "She and her husband were involved in a threesome with another woman, also one of the founders. They were forced to resign."

"Really?" Danni said. "And she didn't even invite you to join in? You definitely must be losing your touch."

"Very funny," Mort said. "As long as I haven't lost it with you."

Danni closed her books, leaned over and put them on the floor, then beckoned to him with her finger.

* * *

Several nights later, after dinner, as the twins clamored for apple sauce and Mort was doing a sloppy job of feeding them, he said to Danni, "When you go to that Slattery appearance next week, I'm going with you. After the show, we'll take a cab uptown, and I'll take you to that 2nd Avenue Deli I told you about. Overpriced, but great sandwiches."

"Hate to burst your bubble, but they moved his show to Florida earlier this year. Broadcasts from a humble, multi-million-dollar condo, as I just found out."

"Florida? I thought they were on Avenue of the Americas," Mort said.

"They are, but when you've attained super-star status, you can apparently go wherever you want. Maybe we can just Zoom the interview."

Thirty-three

And Zoom it was. Danni was on a computer in the second bedroom of their Georgetown condo as she was introduced.

"And with us tonight is Danielle Rose," Sean Slattery said from his home studio in Florida, "a professor of constitutional law from American University Law School in Washington, DC, to talk with us about First Amendment issues. She is a graduate of Syracuse University College of Law and served as law clerk to two federal judges before she became law clerk and subsequently *senior* law clerk to Senior Associate Justice J.J. Richter of the US Supreme Court. Welcome, Professor Rose."

Viewed from the chest up on Zoom, Slattery was wearing a blue suit with the standard bright-red tie. His thick hair was, as usual, parted in the middle, and he was oozing friendliness. Danni, in a colorful summer blouse, was wearing jeans, since the Zoom only captured her from the waist up. The bookcase behind her was filled with texts and a lot of Mort's material. Mort was seated off to the side, out of sight, as were the twins' cribs. The twins were spending the evening in Travilah.

"Good evening, Mr. Slattery. But it's associate professor, and I'm comfortable with Danni."

"Fair enough. I understand that Justice Richter is now your father-in-law, and you are married to the Pulitzer Prize-winning reporter Mort Ahrens of the Washington Post, who, incidentally, just wrote a series on book banning. I appreciate your stepping in after the tragic death of Professor Bickel, who was originally scheduled."

"Thank you. It was a great loss."

"There seems to be a great hue and cry about efforts throughout the country to ban certain books, texts, and materials from schools and libraries. While I appreciate the freedoms of the First Amendment and freedom of speech, don't people have the right to keep improper material out of the hands of children and those unable to discern what is in their best interests?"

"That's really a three-pronged question," Danni said. "First, let's talk about freedom of speech. The First Amendment to our Constitution says that 'Congress shall make no law abridging freedom of speech or of the press.' That, in and of itself, places a huge burden on Congress and protects the freedom of speech and the press. But most of today's attacks on books and publications now come from the states.

"The first case that comes to mind is Bantam Books v. Sullivan, decided back in 1963. In that Rhode Island case, the legislature created a commission to recommend prosecution for publications that were deemed obscene and give protestors the right to circulate lists of offensive books to local police departments accordingly. The Supreme Court, in an eight-to-one decision, determined that this was objectionable and violated not only the First Amendment but also the Fourteenth Amendment, which protects due process of law, because even though the states had the right to regulate obscene materials, it had to be done within a procedural mechanism. Without utilizing those mechanisms, such as a legal hearing, their actions were illegal and unconstitutional."

At this point, Slattery said, "Well, apparently the Supreme Court felt that the states were the first guardians of materials deemed obscene or inappropriate, and as you explained, most of the battles now being fought are on the state level. What has the Supreme Court said since 1963?"

"Interestingly," Danni said, "because it's deemed primarily a matter for the states, the court has basically not taken a position. The seminal case, from 1982, arose from a Long Island case, Board of Education of Island Trees Union Free School District v. Pico, where the school board directed that several books be removed from the shelves of both junior high and high school libraries, including at least one Pulitzer Prize winner. The board felt the designated books were violative of Christian and Jewish beliefs, were anti-Semitic, and to quote, 'just plain filthy.' A group of students appealed that decision, started a lawsuit, and the case eventually reached the Supreme Court. These appeals take years, and a closely divided court held that books can be removed after proper procedural processes only for sound reasons, such as vulgarity or not meeting educational standards. Perhaps, we'll get more definition down the road."

"So, the court got involved at least as far as kicking the problem back to the states," Slattery said.

"Yes, for each case to be decided on community standards. But the problem is, what are community standards, and who is best to determine what they are? There have been attacks on 4,200 books around the country in the last two years, according to the American Library Association, and the courts are filled with cases as a result."

Slattery asked, "So, a school board or a library board can ban certain books, but then it gets tested in the courts?"

Danni nodded. "And according to the Association, the bulk of those complaints have been circulated nationwide by only a very few groups and very few people, then disseminated by social media or newsletters. Which brings us to your second point—people *do* have the right to make those determinations, with a big caveat."

"Which is?"

"While parents have an absolute right to control what their children read, they don't have the right to tell other parents what *their* kids should read. Translate that to school boards, public libraries and the like, and you can see why there is such public arousal. I don't necessarily want *you* to make the choice for *my* children."

Slattery laughed and said, "Fortunately, my children can make their own choices. They're grown, and they can decide for my grandchildren."

"I'm sure they're terrific adults," Danni said, "but I want those same prerogatives for my children. And where you have groups disseminating lists from one community to another, one part of the country to another, without the recipients making an educated determination on their own, this can stifle creativity, education, free expression of ideas, and strike at the heart of democracy itself."

"Isn't that taking it a bit far?" Slattery said.

"I don't think so," Danni answered. "There have been incidents of violence all over the country over books that people want to get banned. They overreact, and damage follows. My husband, Mort, described one such incident in his series of articles, where an attorney who represented a librarian in a book banning case was brutally stabbed to death. A young single mother."

"I read the articles," Slattery said, "and that was a tragedy. But there are unstable people walking the streets all over this country, and those things happen, unfortunately. These are isolated incidents, as I read them."

"Isolated?" Danni said. "Not by a long shot. There have been hundreds, if not thousands of incidents—threats to librarians, school board members and elected officials, to say nothing of people who merely spoke up. Teachers have been fired for allowing their students to sing Somewhere Over the Rainbow, Holocaust books have been banned in some places, as well as Pulitzer Prize winners, and Facebook messages have included death threats to librarians. One teacher received a threat that said, 'you can't hide, we know where you live, you have a bullseye on your back.' Some jurisdictions have authorized fines or even jail terms for whoever they deem to be violators. In some places, pets have mysteriously died or disappeared after warnings."

"As I said, anecdotal," Slattery said. "That's why we have courts."

"Is this an atmosphere that we want to permeate education? A climate of fear? Where even what someone perceives as a mention of sex is deemed pornographic?"

"Anecdotal. I'll keep my faith in the courts and the police," Slattery said.

"Some people will be afraid to let their children outside after a rainstorm for fear that they'll see a rainbow and become tainted."

Slattery laughed.

"Meanwhile, guns are rampant, in practically anyone's hands, which makes it worse," Danni said. "We put restrictions on women's bodies, on so many aspects of life, but we shouldn't stifle education, literature and what this country stands for. What about election workers? Volunteers who just want to make our elections safer. Hundreds of threats have been reported. There have been lawsuits, and in one case a lawyer owes millions of dollars to two election workers he libeled."

"That, I think, is a topic for another discussion," Slattery said, moving quickly to change the subject. "You have been a fascinating and very informed guest. And I want to thank you. Especially, because I'm aware that you stepped in on short notice due of the death of your colleague. You are certainly challenging. I hope you'll come back again."

"Thank you for having me," Danni said. "And I'm sure this was good practice for what I'll face when the students return."

The station immediately went to a commercial.

Thirty-four

Danni's Zoom appearance on the Slattery show took place on Friday night. By Saturday, her phone, and Mort's, was busy all day with congratulatory calls. On Facebook and Twitter, the reaction was mixed—some plaudits and some derogatory dissents.

"You take the bad with the good," Mort said. "Everyone is entitled to their opinion."

They had driven to Travilah to pick up the twins that afternoon and stayed for an early dinner. Just as they finished eating, Mort's phone rang and he picked up.

"Alison," he said. "Surprising that we didn't hear from you all day."

Alison didn't even mention the television appearance. "Mort," she said, "I've got to get out to Kansas. Atticus apparently caught whatever bug struck Eric, and he's really sick. Eric worsened, and they're moving him to Saint Luke Hospital, which is in Shelter Rock. I know it's a small hospital, and frankly, I don't know the degree of their expertise, but he really went downhill this week, so there's little choice. Atticus told me that at least this week's paper is out, but he sounds as sick as a dog, so I'm going to use some personal time. I fly out early tomorrow morning. I emailed Marcie, even though she's not officially back until next week, but you're the next in command, I guess."

"Really sorry to hear about Atticus," Mort said, "and Eric as well. You should get a white hat with a red cross on it. You're becoming a regular Florence Nightingale."

"Who?"

"Florence Nightingale—famous for starting modern nursing. Lived in the 1800s."

"Mort," Alison said, "that memory of yours is out of sight. I don't have a nurse's cap, but he really needs me. I'll call you as soon as I know more."

After Mort disconnected and explained the situation, Chickie said, "You know, she's right. Your memory should be registered as a weapon."

"That's how he won all that money on Jeopardy," Danni said.

"Gimme a break guys," Mort said. "That was Teen Jeopardy and well into the past. Most of that memory is gone with old age."

J.J. laughed. "Old age? You don't know anything about old age. What are you, thirty-five? Wait until your bones fight you when you get out of bed in the morning."

"Another perfect reason why you should retire," Chickie said.

"You see what I have to live with?" J.J. snorted. "She just wants a companion so she can tour the world."

"Get some travel in while you still can," Chickie said. "You can't stand that conservative majority on the court, as it is."

"That's exactly why I have to stay," J.J. said, defending his position. "Somebody has to protect the Constitution. If not me, who?"

"How about the new constitutional scholar?" Mort said. "Danni would be a great justice."

"Couldn't agree more," J.J. said. "And if you can figure out how to get her appointed to the court by this regressive administration, I'll resign tomorrow and become Chickie's aged, full-time companion."

"You already are," Chickie countered. "How do all our conversations eventually get back to the law?" Changing the subject, she said to Danni, "Why don't you two stay over tonight? Give us another night with the twins. Lupe will make us a feast in the morning. She'd love that."

"And Katie would be very happy too," Danni said, "with J.J. to spoil her. Just look at her."

Mort looked at Danni helplessly and shrugged.

"Sold," Danni said.

Katie, who was ensconced on J.J.'s lap, opened a sleepy eye and agreed too.

* * *

While he was seated at the dining room table the following morning, Mort's phone pinged again. Katie, whose loyalty was usually directed to Mort when there was food available, was right at J.J.'s feet. She learned fast.

Mort looked at the screen.

"Alison again," he said, and then picked up. "Alison, where are you?" A long pause. "You're there already? What did you do, fly a cargo plane in the middle of the night?" Another long pause, then Mort said, "I'm going to put you on speakerphone so Danni can catch this. We're still in Travilah with the folks."

He thumbed a button and Alison's voice brightened the room. "As I was saying, I think you should get out here, Mort. The city council apparently is appointing some sort of a 'purity' committee they're going to announce at the regular meeting tomorrow. The conscience police or something. Atticus's ex-wife is somehow involved, if not the instigator. The committee will screen all books in the library and the schools and then impose restrictions. You know, pull some off the shelves. Ban others. Sounds like a perfect follow-up to our series, but I've got my hands full with Atticus. He's really feeling shitty. This thing seems to be affecting his nervous system as well, just like Eric, who is considerably worse and in the hospital. Anyhow, if you think it's a good idea, American has a flight to KC later this afternoon, and you could be here before sundown."

Mort looked at Danni, who gave a thumbs up and mouthed, "I'm going with you."

"Sounds like a plan," Mort said. "And I think Danni is coming with me. We'll see you tonight."

Mort turned to Chickie. "Looks like you've got your wish. You've got the twins for a few more days. I'll get on the horn and get us reservations." Then he turned to Danni and said, "What about your preparation for the constitutional law class?"

"I can read on the plane or in a hotel room. Or Atticus's condo. And I think they're both being poisoned."

"Who?"

"Eric and Atticus. Sounds like thallium poisoning to me. This is getting really frightening."

"Thallium? What's that? And since when do you know poisons?"

"The two of you lost me," Chickie said, "but please explain."

J.J. was listening intently, with Katie on his lap again, saying nothing.

"Hey, Mort," Danni said. "You figured out that bombing in Mississippi, which involved a chemical, didn't you? My turn now. Thallium is a chemical that can be deadly if you ingest a large amount, but if you only get it in smaller doses, it causes vomiting, diarrhea, and particularly hair loss and disorientation. Sounds to me like that's what the two of them are suffering from."

"And where did you get this expertise?"

"In criminal law we spent a couple of days on poisons used in some notable cases. Thallium is called the 'poisoner's poison.' Has chemical and industrial use and throws off the same symptoms that Alison described. It stuck with me in case I ever needed it for a husband," Danni said, throwing a glance at Mort.

"You talk about *my* memory. How many years ago did this casually come up in a law school class? You really think someone is poisoning them? Has this craziness gone that far?"

"I suspect we'll soon find out," Danni said.

Thirty-five

Shelter Rock, Kansas

Thanks to the heads-up from Alison, Danni and Mort were back in Atticus's second bedroom by Sunday evening. Atticus was at home with Alison. As reported, he looked like hell. Alison had reported Danni's suspicions about thallium poisoning to the resident physician on duty at Saint Luke Hospital, and although the theory was met with skepticism, several of the doctors discussed the possibility and decided that thallium poisoning was a distinct possibility.

The medical staff had even gone so far as referring to their medical texts and had become more convinced. In their review of thallium as a weapon of destruction, the texts had revealed that it had been used in marital disputes, by heads of state against opponents or enemies, in custody cases, and even against a reporter in a European country famous for that kind of conduct.

As the medical staff's research uncovered, the only antidote approved by the FDA in cases of thallium poisoning was a substance called Prussian blue, which binds to the intestinal tract and dissipates the damage. Van Gogh had used it as a colorization in some of his paintings. Available only by prescription, it was still in use in the bluing of textiles. Prussian blue is a pigment which traps thallium in the intestines and keeps it from being absorbed into the body. Unfortunately, it was not available in a small city like Shelter Rock in the middle of Kansas, but the doctors quickly determined they could get some from a hospital in Kansas City.

Atticus immediately said, "I can fly to KC tomorrow morning and pick it up. Should be back before noon if they can have someone meet me at the airport." The resident intern at the hospital, Dr. Chang Wang, made the arrangements. Literally, the dye was set. Alison stayed behind to prepare for Monday night's city council meeting. Danni said she would stay, too, and do some reading up on Alison and Mort's research and reports. Mort, the only member of the quartet who had not yet flown with Atticus, was happy to accompany him on the trip to Kansas City.

Atticus said, "Make sure they'll have someone meet us at Wheeler Downtown Airport, and not at the International Airport." Dr. Wang said that he would do that.

Eric Robbins was in intensive care, but he perked up when he heard that Danni's suspicions might lead to a solution for the illnesses. Eric looked shrunken in the bed, having lost most of his thinning hair. His skin almost matched the color of his hospital gown.

* * *

At dinner time, Mort, who was still excited for his first plane ride with Atticus, was dispatched in their rental car to Gambino's Pizza on Main Street and picked up two large pizzas for dinner. Atticus retched when they opened the first box and said he would stick with tea and crackers until his digestive system returned to normal.

As they sat around the table, Danni said, "The question is, who was trying to poison you two, and why?"

"That's the funny part," Atticus said, "because Eric and I really didn't spend any time together other than when I was at the paper. We didn't share any meals, and none of the women at the Clarion got ill, so it's not as though the workplace was infected."

"Did you share *anything*?" Mort asked.

Atticus paused, then snapped his fingers. "Donuts! We shared donuts a few times. In Eric's office. He loves donuts. Didn't even offer them to the ladies out front. Father Hoffmann, the priest, dropped them off."

"Poisoned donuts?" Mort said. "Sounds like an Agatha Christie plot."

Danni said, "That's what they did in several of the poisoning cases we studied. Sprinkled a little thallium on the donuts, and it's practically undetectable. There was one case where a woman was breaking up with her boyfriend and poured a big dose into his milk shake. It killed him."

"Where did the donuts come from?" Mort asked. "Is there a donut store owner who dislikes Eric so much that he'd try to kill him?"

"I don't think anyone dislikes him that much," Atticus said. "But Father Hoffmann stopped in with donuts every few days to see Eric. He's been doing that ever since Eric's mother died. That's where the donuts came from, and I had a few bites."

"The priest?" Alison said. "You're suggesting the priest is a poisoner? C'mon."

"That priest, Father Hoffmann," Atticus said, "is deeply involved with my ex-wife. I've heard it so many times that I think people are anxious to have me confront her about the relationship. But fortunately, she's out of my life. And she's become essential to Families for Freedom. She's the editor of their newsletter and wrote that letter to the *Post* that you guys sent me. She was always an evangelical, and very into the church, so I can see her getting on board with perceived sin and book banning. But sprinkling poison on donuts seems like A Bridge Too Far, to use a movie reference."

"I loved that film," Mort said, smiling.

"Mort!" Danni admonished.

Atticus said, "I think there might have been some donuts left in the box, come to think of it. Stale by now. Eric got really sick and so did I, but I only had a few bites. They should be sitting in a box in his office."

"I think we should get the police involved before we start playing sleuth," Mort said.

"You want to ask the professionals, instead of jumping in headfirst?" Danni said. "Now that's a switch."

"Val Cummings? The police chief?" Alison said. "I wouldn't trust him as far as I could throw him. And I couldn't."

"Good point," Atticus said, "but Sheriff Hakim Melendez is a straight shooter. I trust him. I've even taken him flying several times when he had to get to a scene in a hurry. We could ask him to get the donuts tested, if there are any left in the box. I'm sure he'd do it."

Mort looked at Atticus and said, " Would the priest go that far? I find it hard to believe."

Atticus shook his head. "I don't trust any of these people, although I can't get my head around the thought that Tish or Father Hoffmann would go that far. But before we get ahead of ourselves, where would Father Hoffmann get thallium? I doubt that anyone around here carries it. And it's an unlikely drug for the local pharmacies. Nobody around here would use it."

They left it as a question to be decided. Atticus and Mort drove to the *Clarion* after they finished their meal. Because of Eric's illness, Atticus had a key. Sure enough, there were three donuts left in the box in Eric's office. As they were carefully wrapping the donuts, they heard a woman's loud voice from outside the office. Mort looked out the front window and saw one woman walking on the sidewalk. He looked puzzled.

"Is she talking to herself?" Mort asked.

Atticus laughed. "Yes, she is. That's Jennie Smith. She's harmless, but she has some… problems. She hangs around the church and dotes on Father Hoffmann."

They took the donuts back to Atticus's condo and on Monday morning delivered them with an explanation to Sheriff Hakim Melendez.

Melendez was very reluctant to get involved. He didn't want to step on the toes of a fellow law officer but agreed to have the donuts tested by his forensic staff and then discuss next steps. He said he found the theory that a priest could be attempting to murder someone hard to believe.

Thirty-six

The city council met every other Monday in city hall in room 203. The meeting was presided over by the Mayor, David Fielder, with the four council members present. Public attendance at the meetings was sporadic. When there was a controversy or a topic of great importance, more people showed up. Such was the case as Danni, Mort, Alison and Atticus crowded into the room with all seats filled and some people standing. City employees were present, seated in front of the mayor and council members, as well as Chief Val Cummings. Cummings did a double take when he saw Alison.

Mayor Fielder had long feuded with the *Clarion* and the way it covered city government. The recently deceased Margery Robbins had made a point of attending every meeting and publishing her criticisms of what she characterized as "favoritism, nepotism, ultra-conservatism and questionable ethics" of the entire city government. She was particularly harsh about the mayor and objected to many of his "official" acts as self-serving, illegal and smacking of conflict of interest.

David Fielder was the proprietor of Fielder's Foods, by far the largest grocery store in Shelter Rock. It had a very popular bakery department where residents could purchase rolls, cakes, pies, donuts, even fresh bagels. Eric had recently written a scathing editorial about Fielder who had gotten the city council to block an application for a new bakery in town on very technical alleged ordinance violations.

Of the four city council members, three inevitably voted with him, and one, Jeannette O'Connor, a Native American, reliably opposed the majority. Jeanette was also the sister of Agnes, one of the employees of the *Clarion*.

Mayor Fielder frequently accused the paper of outright lies and often criticized it on his personal Facebook page. He was particularly demeaning to Margery, though generally less hostile to her son, Eric, who now served as both publisher and editor. Margery had often accused the council of holding illegal meetings or "secret sessions," as she described them, in violation of KOMA (Kansas Open Meetings Act), a statute enacted to ensure all meetings would be open to the public.

Public reaction to the raid on the *Clarion* had reverberated throughout the entire county, and even critics of the paper were appalled at the conduct that accompanied the raid. Both the prosecutor who compiled the information leading to the search warrant and the local judge who signed the warrant had resigned in the past month, and those offices were still not filled. Mayor Fielder had asked them not to resign, but the public outcry over their conduct and the adverse publicity were just too much. The police chief, as he had told Alison during their interview, said that he was "only doing his job and carrying out the mandate of the court," but he did apologize for an "overreaction" on the part of some of his part-time officers. He blamed it on "inexperience."

When Mayor Fielder convened the meeting, the first order of business was the salute to the flag, with everyone standing, hand over heart, and reciting the pledge of allegiance. The meeting was then called to order, the minutes of the last meeting were approved, and the standard approval of warrants, salaries and other procedural matters passed unanimously. There was a discussion of the next year's budget, a report from the city engineer about an airport runway repair, cursory discussion of a mobile food vendor ordinance, which was tabled, and a report on pending litigation, the only item of which was the lawsuit against the police department by the *Clarion* employee whose hand was broken in the raid.

The mayor ended the public session by saying, "We will now adjourn for thirty minutes for an executive session to discuss with the city attorney several proposals to be brought up in the public portion of the meeting to follow."

"That," Atticus said, leaning over to Danni and Alison, "is one of the things that bugged the hell out of Margery. She felt that the law required that these matters be discussed in public. She often wrote about it but never took it further." During the break, Atticus spotted his ex-wife, Tish, entering the room, and pointed her out. Tish was dressed smartly in a summer suit and carried a sheaf of papers.

When the council returned, the mayor said, "We will now consider a proposal from Ms. Tish Duvall to have the Ten Commandments prominently displayed in every classroom in the district, as has become the practice in several other jurisdictions, and which is a growing trend. Ms. Duvall, who is an administrator in our school district, also has another proposal on the agenda this evening regarding scrutiny of books and literature in the schools to keep lewd, pornographic and inappropriate material out of the hands of our children, as noted in the items of business before us."

He gestured for Tish to take the floor.

"Tell me this wasn't planned well in advance," Atticus whispered.

Before his ex-wife had a chance to speak, Atticus rose, raised his hand and said, in a powerful voice, "Excuse me."

"Sir?"

"Not sir, Mr. Mayor, you know me well. I'm Atticus Duvall, a faculty member at John F. Kennedy Grammar School, and I'd like to know if Ms. Duvall has the permission of the school board to make this proposal. This is the first I've heard of it, and—"

"You're out of order, Mr. Duvall," Mayor Fielder said.

Danni rose to her feet, all five-foot-two of her, and raised a hand.

"Uh oh," Mort said to Alison. "I think the shit is about to hit the fan."

"Ma'am?" Mayor Fielder said.

"I believe that what Mr. Duvall is raising is a point of order, and a point of order takes precedence."

"And you are?"

"Danielle Rose."

"And are you a member of this community?" Mayor Fielder asked.

"No, I am not, but I am representing Mr. Duvall."

Atticus looked on bemused.

"Are you a member of the bar?" Mayor Fielder asked, now confused as to how to proceed.

"I am an Associate Professor at American University Law School, admitted to practice before the United States Supreme Court, the US District of Columbia Court of Appeals, the US District Court in Washington, DC, the US Second Circuit Court of Appeals, the bar of the State of Maryland, the bar of the State of New York, and have been admitted *Pro Haec Vice* in the State of Delaware. And once again, a point of order takes precedence. Please ask your counsel."

Every eye in the room was now fixed on Danni, who stood defiant with her chin jutting out. Mayor Fielder looked thoroughly flummoxed. He turned and leaned over to the city attorney, a local *Barney Fife* look-alike coincidentally named Barney Pennington, who was the son of the recently resigned judge. They whispered a few words to each other and then the mayor turned back to Danni.

"I guess you can speak, then. And what is the point of order?" Mayor Fielder asked weakly.

"What Mr. Duvall was saying," Danni explained, "or actually, was about to say, was that before Ms. Duvall can make a proposal to hang the Ten Commandments in every classroom—and I might add, which version of the Ten Commandments was not mentioned, to say nothing of the constitutional guarantees afforded in matters involving church and state—she *must* have the concurrence or approval of the school board or education board before this body can consider such a proposal."

Tish Duvall remained standing, furiously ruffling her papers during this exchange.

Mayor Fielder turned to Tish Duvall. "And do you have such approval?"

Tish spat out her answer. "Not yet, Mr. Mayor. The next board meeting is in August. But this is so pro forma—it's a recognition of

God and country, no different from the Pledge of Allegiance. Louisiana, among other states, just adopted such a ruling."

"And that ruling was immediately challenged in federal court," Danni said, "by the American Civil Liberties Union and several other organizations."

Mayor Fielder again looked at the city attorney, who nodded in accord.

Mayor Fielder took a more sheepish approach. "Ms. Duvall, under the circumstances, I think we will have to table your proposal until you get approval of the board. You do have another item on the agenda, which we will get to next. But first, I think this a good time for us to take another short break."

He looked at the members of the council who questioned him with their eyes but nodded approval.

Thirty-seven

During the council's break, several people went out to have cigarettes while others mixed and talked. It was almost like opposing teams taking opposite sides at a sporting event. Tish Duvall, and those who were sympathetic to her, gathered on one side of the room, glaring at Atticus and his contingent, especially Danni, on the other side of the room.

Several people came over to shake Atticus's hand and converse. They asked to be introduced to Danni and Mort, who were unknown to most of them. They were particularly anxious to converse with Danni after her knowledge of *Robert's Rules of Order* and parliamentary procedure had taken control of the proceedings. It seemed as though many of them already knew Alison, or knew of her. Atticus was clearly very popular with the city folk.

After about fifteen minutes, the council members reappeared and took their seats.

"We will now proceed with the balance of the public portion of the meeting," Mayor Fielder said. "The next item of business, as you can see from the printed schedule, is the proposal from Ms. Duvall to have us appoint a committee—a bipartisan committee, if you will—to scrutinize books and literature in our schools and to remove material that is not suitable for students for various reasons. Ms. Duvall…?"

Tish Duvall once again rose from her seat and moved to the front of the room where the city clerk handed her a microphone. She spoke, but her voice did not carry to the speakers, and she shook the mic. The city clerk got up, pointed to the on/off switch, and she proceeded.

"This proposal," she said, glaring in Danni's direction, "*has* been approved by the school board at its last meeting, so let's get that out of the way right off the bat. It has come to our attention, as it has in so many places throughout this nation, that a great amount of content in books and literature is unfortunately available to our children in the form of lewd, pornographic, obscene or inappropriate material that is antagonistic to a Christian society, or to one who believes in Judeo-Christian beliefs and teachings. We propose the establishment, by this body, of a commission to be named by the council to examine not only materials available in our school libraries, but to scrutinize these materials before they are placed on the shelves, thereby eliminating impurities from damaging young and susceptible minds. While we have not suggested a name, it could operate as a purity council, if you will, in the best traditions of democracy."

"Does this proposal include the public library as well?" Mayor Fielder inquired.

"That," Tish said, "would be a matter for the library board, but I submit that it certainly is a good idea. Certain books should not be in the hands of our children before a certain age, and some, I submit, should not be in anyone's hands at all, because of their lewd, lascivious and obscene nature. But I am only suggesting, or this proposal is only suggesting, I should say, control of our school libraries."

"And how would the council appoint this commission?" The mayor asked.

"What we discussed at the board meeting was that interested parties would submit their names to the city council, which would then select three, or perhaps five individuals to make up the committee. The committee would meet regularly, perhaps right here in this chamber—open and public meetings—primarily to consider citizen objections to books and render its determination. If the book, or material, was considered unsuitable or inappropriate, it would be removed from school shelves."

The mayor asked, "And if such a determination was made, what recourse would be available to other citizens who didn't agree, or perhaps even to authors or publishers?"

"Well, it might be that the city council itself would be the final arbiter, and of course the courts."

"Anything else?"

"No," Tish said. "That would be the gist of it."

"Well, then, let's open the floor for discussion," the mayor suggested. "Raise your hand if you wish to be heard, then come forward to the microphone that's in the center aisle. Ms. Duvall, please remain right where you are."

A half dozen hands went up. One by one, people gave opinions. Several spoke uncomfortably, clearly not used to public speaking. One lady said, "Isn't this a violation of the freedom of speech, which I think is in the First Amendment?"

"No," Tish Duvall said, "because we have built in an appeal process so that due process is protected. This is not censorship, mind you, it is merely to keep unsuitable materials from the hands of our students."

The woman said, "Oh," and returned to her seat.

Other questions involved how the committee would be selected, whether three or five members was a suitable number, how notice of the meetings would be conducted.

Danni's hand was one of those raised, and as others spoke, she was the last one recognized.

"Mrs....?" the mayor said, not recalling her last name.

"Rose," Danni said. "And yes, I am a missus. My husband is right here," she said, pointing to Mort.

"And are you speaking again in behalf of Mr. Duvall?" the mayor asked.

"Yes, I am."

Atticus stood and shook his head in affirmation.

"Ms. Duvall," Danni said, "or is it Mrs.?"

Tish smiled with saccharin sweetness and said, "You can just call me Tish."

"Fine. Now, Tish, you talked about inappropriate material, but you never defined what you considered to be inappropriate. And you talked about control of libraries. Could you explain that a little better?"

"Not fit for the hands or minds of our children," Tish said, "books that would not be appropriate—you know, lewd and obscene."

"Yes, you already said that several times," Danni said. "But let's get a little more specific. Books that contain material about homosexuality, for instance?"

"Yes. Children or students don't need to read that trash in school."

"But if their parents felt that discussions or material about homosexuality was appropriate in the home, you wouldn't object?" Danni asked.

"I can't control what other people do in their homes," Tish said. "But not *my* children, and not in *my* home. That's part of the depravity that marks the disintegration of our culture."

"Oh, and how many children do you have?" Danni asked, already knowing the answer.

"The Lord has not yet blessed me in that regard," Tish said, "but someday, I hope. It was merely a figure of speech."

"Let's move on," Danni said, "and I'll give you some examples so you can just say either 'appropriate' or 'inappropriate.' That should be easier. LBGTQ topics?"

"Inappropriate."

"Anything about transgender individuals or their medical treatment would be inappropriate, then?"

"Absolutely."

"Abortion. Even scientific information."

"Definitely inappropriate."

"Contraception, In Vitro Fertilization or IVF?"

"Also inappropriate, and birth control as well, before you ask me."

"Drug use, heroin, fentanyl, even marijuana, other drugs?"

"Inappropriate. Drugs are one of the scourges of our society."

"Same sex marriage?"

"Inappropriate."

"Marriages between people of different races?"

"Inappropriate. That's one of the things that's diluting the purity of our race."

"Really? You had better discuss that with one of our Supreme Court Justices," Danni said.

Tish glared.

"The sanctity of marriage? Adultery?"

Tish glared at Danni. "I feel as if I'm being cross-examined," she said. "Adultery, that's one of the prohibitions of the Ten Commandments. Of course it's sacred."

"Fair enough," Danni said. "I'm told that you are a member of Families for Freedom, is that correct? Is that where these beliefs and ideas for a purity commission originated?"

"Yes, I am a member, and proudly so. And I am the editor of the organization's newsletter of which I believe you are well aware, but if you must know, this came to me from the voice of God. God spoke to me and chose me to help resanctify the world gone astray. These are Christian principles and Christian beliefs, and I make no apology for that. It was the voice of God."

At this point, a woman in the fourth row rose and pointed a finger at Tish Duvall. Jennie Smith was a small woman, about fifty, with stringy brown hair and no makeup. She had a large cross hanging from a chain and had been muttering quietly during the questioning.

"You are a liar!" she shouted. "A sinner! God would *never speak to you!*"

Every eye in the room focused on Jennie. She swayed with the emotion of her words, her face red with anger, veins bulging in her neck. Jennie Smith was well-known in Shelter Rock. She had limited education, did odd jobs around the city, lived alone, and was the caretaker of the St. John Nepomucene Catholic church. She spent much of her time in the church, day and night, not only for prayer, but to keep it in pristine condition. In her view, being in church also allowed her to be closer to her God.

"You defiled Father Hoffmann. You led him away from his vows! Don't think I haven't seen you with him, both of you 'nekid' in sin. In God's house! You are a vixen!"

The room erupted in chaos.

Thirty-eight

The two couples sat on the patio near the firepit behind Atticus's condo. A bottle of Centenario Grande Reserva 2022 was almost empty. Mort held his glass up to the sunlight and twirled it.

"Dark and delicious," he said. "I didn't know that the Portuguese made such great wines."

"The Douro Valley has some great wineries," Atticus said. "You should visit sometime."

Danni was clad in shorts, running shoes and a T-shirt. She had just gotten back from her daily two- to three-mile jog. It was early afternoon.

"We are cursed when it comes to vacationing," Danni said. "Mort got yanked from our honeymoon cruise in Central America after two days. No matter what is planned, Mort runs into a crisis at work and it goes up in flames. Alison can confirm that."

"Wait a minute, professor," Mort said. "Whose promotion loused up our latest plans?"

"Okay. One for you," Danni said. "But a half dozen for me. No contest."

"By the way," Mort said, "I spoke with the paper this morning, and we've got additional time to wrap up this stay and get a good article. I also spoke with Chickie, and she's thrilled to have the kids for some extra time."

"Thanks for sharing," Danni said.

"How about we delve into today's debacle?" Alison said.

"Fair enough. But I find it difficult to believe that Tish, of all people, could get herself involved with the priest," Atticus said. "I mean, she always was flirtatious. But the priest allowing it to happen? That's hard to accept."

"Well, apparently she found something hard," Mort said, smiling.

"Mort!" Danni said.

"Now there's a side of Mort I never saw before," Alison said. "The sexual joker."

"That woman making the accusations at the meeting last night certainly brought things to a calamitous end," Danni said. "Do you think she was being truthful?"

"Jennie Smith, by her reputation, doesn't know how to lie," Atticus said. "She's super-religious, but not in an evangelical way. She's like married to the Church. If she's not cleaning the place up, she's praying. Wanders around town sort of talking to herself, does odd jobs here and there, but literally is married to the Church. Like the priest should be. She'd never lie about anything like that. In fact, I'll bet she doesn't lie period. And Tish ran out of that council meeting so fast she could have broken the record for the hundred meters."

"It just proves that you never know," Alison said. "And she certainly looked at me with disapproval, as though she still has a say in Atticus's life."

"Okay," Mort said, "now that we've digested all this, and the prurient side of Shelter Rock, let's get back to the criminal side. If that priest did the actual thallium sprinkling of the donuts, we're talking serious criminal conduct. Why? That's a lot worse than a sexual indiscretion. And I have to wonder—did Father Hoffmann use condoms?"

Danni screamed. "Morton! Enough!"

Atticus snickered. "Well, Tish did say that God hadn't favored her with children… yet. Getting it on with the priest is certainly trying to get closer to God, no?"

Danni couldn't help but laugh, along with Alison. She looked at Mort and Atticus. "You two are a great pair. Maybe you should take this act out on the road. But getting back to the main point, what do we do if the donuts turn up poisoned?"

"It's already in the hands of the sheriff. Let him take it from there," Mort said. "He's got to proceed, one way or another. I don't know about jurisdiction, between him and the police chief, but I'd guess that one of them will have to file charges."

* * *

On Tuesday morning the sheriff confirmed that the donuts had been tainted with thallium. He was extremely uncomfortable about having been put in this position, but said he would go forward and launch a complete investigation and bring Father Hoffmann in for questioning. He did have concurrent jurisdiction with the police chief of any crimes committed in the county.

It developed that it was just as well that the matter rested with the sheriff. He made an appointment with Father Hoffmann to come in on Tuesday afternoon—for an interview—but also went to the county prosecutor, since the city office was vacant because of the recent resignation, to get a search warrant for the priest's office and quarters. He was extremely uncomfortable doing so and regretted that he had gotten involved.

* * *

Father Hoffmann stopped in on Tuesday morning at Fielder's Foods, as was his usual practice, and had his usual cup of coffee with Mayor Fielder before visiting ailing parishioners and other people in need.

"I have an interview with Sheriff Melendez later this afternoon," he told the mayor, "although I don't for the life of me understand why. He said it was something to do with an ongoing investigation. He had no specifics, and I certainly have my hands full at the moment because of what happened last evening at the council meeting."

"I hesitated to bring it up," the mayor said, "but Jennie created chaos, and it brought our meeting to a sudden halt."

"Well, I will have to get to Wichita later in the week for a session with the bishop. I need to get this straightened out. This whole dustup was terribly unsettling, to say the least."

"Very embarrassing."

Father Hoffmann nodded and said, "Embarrassing for you, humiliating for me. Jennie has had visions in the past, people tell me, but this was beyond anything I could have imagined. It's true that Tish Duvall and I are very fond of one another, almost like brother and sister, but I have one sister in Florida and that's quite enough, to be honest. True, also, that Tish and I have spent an inordinate amount of time together because of her devotion to Families for Freedom, and with my blessings, I might add.

"By the way, about that prescription I got from my brother-in-law for you. Has it been helpful in your scientific endeavors?"

Mayor Fielder blanched. "Umm, yes—it was just what was needed."

* * *

Father Hoffmann showed up on time for the interview with the sheriff, as was his habit. He was surprised to see a stenographer and a video recorder in the room. What he failed to know was that the sheriff had obtained a search warrant from the county prosecutor, and at that very moment investigators were at the church searching his quarters.

Thirty-nine

The questioning of Father Hoffmann was routine. Name, address, background, length of time as a priest, various parishes served, how long he'd been in Shelter Rock, et cetera.

"This is all pretty mundane," Father Hoffmann said. "I imagine you had something else in mind when you asked me here. You said something about an ongoing investigation, so…?"

"True enough," Sheriff Melendez said. "Part of my job requires touching all the bases and getting the routine material recorded. Now, as part of your duties as a priest, I understand that you have a regular schedule of visiting with parishioners, members of the community, people who are ill, and so on. Am I correct?"

"Absolutely," Father Hoffmann said. "It's an important part of my job. But I'm not restricted to members of my parish. In a small community like this, we get to know almost everyone, and we care for them all as well. My duties often take me outside the confines of the church."

"Even to people whose beliefs or whose conduct differs from your own?"

"Again, absolutely. God encompasses us all, not just those who share our beliefs."

"And in that regard," the sheriff said, "you have been regularly visiting with Eric Robbins, the owner of the Clarion, is that correct? And if I'm not mistaken, Robbins family members have been harsh critics of the Church as well as other aspects of government and the community. Would you agree?"

"That's true, which is unique, I suppose—the ability to differ and still break bread, so to speak. However, the Robbinses are also congregants."

"As I understand it, some of your homilies were very pointed in regard to positions the Clarion took on the banning of books, or censorship, as we've come to know it," Sheriff Melendez said.

"Not my homilies, Sheriff, which are more focused on scripture. But my sermons occasionally took issue with some of their editorial positions. We have differed on societal issues, yes, but Eric and his family—his late mother—have been members of our parish longer than I have. A healthy discourse would be a more appropriate description of those sermons."

"And in that regard, again, I understand that it has been your habit to drop off donuts during your visits?"

"Eric and his family have gone through a terrible tragedy recently. First, that raid on his newspaper, and the damage it did, which apparently had questionable justification, and which I spoke about from the pulpit. Then followed the death of his beloved mother only a day later. She was a pillar of strength. Sadly, I presided over her service. Yes, even though we had differences, when I learned of his passion for sweets, I would drop off a box of donuts on my visits as a token of sympathy and to help with his healing. God doesn't play favorites."

"And if I told you," the sheriff said, "that those donuts contained a poison that almost killed him as well as another person, how would you respond?"

The priest appeared to be shocked. After a long pause, he said, "I would be dumbfounded that such a thing could happen. It must be a mistake."

"No mistake. Forensics has confirmed the poisonous substance. I'm not going to arrest you at this time, but this raises serious issues," Sheriff Melendez said. "If you were not a priest, I would say we have more than enough for probable cause. But I know you, and I know where I can reach you, so please remain available while we sort this out. You might also want to consider speaking to an attorney, however.

Would you care to tell me where you got those donuts? Is there a third party involved?"

Father Hoffmann sat back silently and put his hands over his eyes. "I think I had best say no more at the moment. Am I free to leave?"

"At the moment, yes, unless there is something you wish to add."

Hoffmann shook his head. With that, the interview came to an end.

* * *

Father Hoffmann returned to the church and immediately learned—from a very disturbed Jennie Smith—that deputies from the sheriff's office had executed a search of the premises and his personal belongings in the rectory, which adjoined the church.

He knew he had been misled by a request for an official interview while the warrant was being executed.

Hoffmann knew who he had to contact immediately. He called Fielder's Foods. David Fielder was not there. He called Fielder's home and the call went to voicemail. He tried to contact Tish Duvall several times with the same result. Tish was almost always available, so that was just another complication in an already traumatic day. He tried again. Same result. It was imperative that he reach Tish.

It was Tuesday, and Father Hoffmann was scheduled to conduct an evening service at a quarter to seven. During the half hour before services, confessions were usually taken. Services during the week were not well attended, but there were certain people, like Jennie Smith, who he knew would be in attendance. As he slipped into the confessional booth at a quarter past six, the church was deserted.

Father Hoffmann sat on his side of the confessional booth hidden from penitents by a curtain. In a large community, or in a church with a large number of parishioners, the penitent could very well be unknown to the priest. In larger congregations, there was more than one priest. Such was not the case in Shelter Rock.

A man entered the confessional and knelt.

"In the name of the Father and the Son and the Holy Spirit. Amen," Father Hoffmann said.

The man in the confessional responded, "Amen," and then continued. "Bless me, Father, for I have sinned. It has been several years since my last confession."

Father Hoffmann instantly recognized the voice.

The penitent continued. "I have taken the name of the Lord in vain. I have been intemperate. I have borne false witness, and I have harmed my fellow man. I detest this conduct for these sins offend God, and with His help and grace, I will do penance and reform my life."

Father Hoffmann said, "You must refrain from sin, pray for forgiveness, do good works for humankind, and get help so that you can better understand your conduct. And—how have you harmed your fellow man?"

The penitent paused, struggling for words. "I have been untruthful and have obtained a deadly substance, giving it to a fellow man. Damn it, Father, you *know* what I did. I poisoned someone, but I never intended to kill him. I just wanted him to suffer as he has made me suffer. He made my family suffer with his sharp words. How can I do penance and reform my life? I am sorry for my sins and must make it right. Help me!"

"Your act of contrition must include acts that will restore the victim of your sins to health, and then embark on a life free from sin…" And here Father Hoffmann slipped and said, "David. You must take these inappropriate acts to the appropriate authorities before we can talk of penance and absolution."

"Damn it, Father," David Fielder moaned, "I can't do that. It will destroy my wife, my family, the business, my standing in the community—everything I've worked for. No, I cannot." And with that he burst out of the confessional and left the church.

Forty

The following morning, Sheriff Melendez said to Nigel Norcross, the county prosecutor, "I am at a dead end. The search at the rectory turned up nothing that will help us."

At sixty, Nigel Norcross was a bearded and bald man, thin as a rail. He had been the county prosecutor for decades. He was known as "No Nonsense Nigel," a law-and-order prosecutor. He routinely asked the court for maximum sentences, no matter the crime or the circumstances. For that, he was routinely reelected.

"Don't forget, the chain of custody for those donuts was nonexistent. They were brought to you by persons who might have contaminated those donuts themselves. But bringing poisonous donuts to a man who was antagonistic to his church, if Father Hoffmann did this, is a heinous crime," Norcross responded. "We're lucky he didn't kill everyone at the paper. Is he some kind of fiend? Does he have a history? Psychiatric problems? We'll find the answer, because we have no choice but to charge him. The available evidence certainly points to him. Pick him up and bring him in. Maybe he'll say ten 'Hail Marys' and it will go away. I'll notify Judge Robertson in district court. She's the one who signed the warrant."

* * *

Father Hoffmann, distraught over the episode with Mayor Fielder in the confessional, managed to struggle through the evening service and finally reached Tish Duvall by phone.

"Are you all right?" he asked. "Where are you? I've been trying to reach you all day."

"I'm in Wichita. At a motel," Tish said. "I just had to get out of Shelter Rock. You heard what happened last night? I almost had a breakdown. In front of the city council, no less. That woman saw us, and by now I'm sure it's the talk of the whole community. And we've been so careful. Once you leave the church and we relocate, it will all go away, I know. But at the moment, it's a disaster for both of us."

"At the moment, my love, that is not the worst of my problems."

"What could be worse than that?"

"The sheriff thinks I poisoned Eric Robbins. I'm pretty sure I'm going to be charged with a crime."

"Poisoned? Robbins? That's ridiculous. Where did he get that idea?"

"Not as ridiculous as it sounds," Father Hoffmann said. "Apparently, donuts I gave to Eric were laced with some kind of poison. The man almost died. Your ex-husband ate some and was also very ill."

"Well, *that* would be no loss. Too bad he didn't eat more. He's been nothing but aggravation to me… and with that new whore of his, to boot. But how can they charge you if you didn't do it?"

"Tish, you must not speak ill of Atticus or that woman in that way," Hoffmann said. "That is a sin by itself. And yes, I can be charged and probably will be."

"Then, tell the truth and it will go away," Tish said. "No one would believe you committed a crime."

"It's not as simple as that."

"Why not?"

"Because I learned the truth during a confession. And the confessional is sacred."

"Who was it?"

"Don't you understand? I can't disclose what I learned during a confession. It's inviolable, a sacramental seal that cannot be broken."

"But if you're leaving the priesthood, what difference does it make?"

"I can never break that vow, do you understand? *Never* break the seal of a confession."

"Then tell me who it is. I'll be the bad guy," Tish said.

"I can't do that," Father Hoffmann said. He could feel Tish's temperature rising over the phone.

Exasperated, she shouted, "This is bullshit! More of your religious dogma bullshit. You'd destroy all that we have for a stupid rule that's probably four hundred years old? Is that what you're telling me?"

With a trembling voice, Father Hoffmann said, "Tish, please, I can leave the priesthood, but I cannot leave God."

She hung up.

* * *

Sheriff Melendez contacted Father Hoffmann the following morning and told him of the prosecutor's decision to prosecute. He arranged to have the priest arraigned at four the following afternoon when there would be few people around.

"You know, Father," the sheriff said, "this can all go away if the source was someone other than you. You know that, right?"

"Yes, I do know that, Sheriff," Father Hoffmann said. "And I appreciate your consideration, but I cannot do that. There are ecumenical reasons involved."

"Well, you know Norcross and his reputation," Sheriff Melendez said. "He's not one to extend any sympathy. Even to a man of the cloth."

"I'll have to trust in the goodness of God."

"Well, tell God to recommend a good lawyer. Because that's what you'll need. No one here in Shelter Rock is up to the task. But I can recommend a good criminal lawyer from Wichita, if you like."

"Please," Hoffmann said.

* * *

Roger Polk was a stocky sixty-five-year-old with a bushy beard and graying hair. Despite the summer heat, he was wearing a vested suit when he met Father Hoffmann at the entrance of the Marion County District Court at three the following afternoon. Polk had handled criminal cases in his forty years of practice including interactions with local courts all the way up to the US Supreme Court. He shook the priest's hand, and they went into one of the conference rooms.

Father Hoffmann had not described the charges other than to say that they were criminal and very serious. Polk had already checked with the court and learned that among the charges was attempted murder. They had not discussed a fee.

"You are being charged by a criminal information and not by an indictment," Polk explained.

"Does that make a difference?"

"Not really. It just means that no grand jury sat and handed down an indictment. The complaint is drawn in the name of the county sheriff."

"Sheriff Melendez has been very understanding," Father Hoffmann said. "He's the one who recommended you as an attorney."

"I know, and having a complaining witness recommend defense counsel is highly unusual. He must believe in you. So, let's talk about the charges," Polk said.

"I'm innocent of these charges, perhaps naïve as well. To begin, I regularly visit parishioners and members of the community. Perhaps you're familiar with the search at the Shelter Rock Clarion conducted by the authorities?"

"I think the entire country is aware of it," Polk said. "It was clearly an unconstitutional outrage. But how has that resulted in charging you with attempted murder?"

"As part of my daily rounds, I recently visited with the proprietor of the paper, Eric Robbins, who recently lost his mother on top of some other traumas. I brought him the gift of some donuts. They were provided to me by someone else specifically for Eric, a fact I never mentioned to Eric. I had no reason to suspect that the donuts were apparently poisoned. My naivety is that when I was told not to identify they were provided by a third party, I suspected nothing but a desire for anonymity."

"If that's the case," Polk said, "and you had no knowledge of the criminal intent, or that they were poisoned, you are no more than an innocent third party. When we make that disclosure to the court, the charges should be dismissed. Where did you get the donuts?"

"That's the problem," the priest said. "I learned of this deception during a confession directly to me. As you know, as a priest, I cannot disclose anything I learned during a confession."

Polk crossed himself. "Houston, we have a problem," he said. "But there is more than one way to skin this cat, to abuse an overused metaphor. We just have to trace the origin of the poison, and that will point us in the direction of your freedom. I understand your problem, and the sanctity of the confession, although I am not a Catholic."

"That's not it exactly," Father Hoffmann said, "because I gave the poison to the man who was poisoned. Unwittingly, yes, but I'm also the person who had obtained it. I got it at his request, under what I now know were false pretenses, from someone out of state. Clearly, the intent was to poison the recipient, but I had no knowledge of that. Actually, I had no reason to suspect anything until the confession."

"Ah, so the plot thickens," Polk said. "Without violating the terms of the confession, can you explain to me where this poisonous material came from?"

"It was mailed to me from Florida. I had no idea, in fact, that it was a poison."

"Florida? An interstate transaction. Another complication. If it crossed state lines, we're talking about a probable federal prosecution, not a state one. But don't worry, I'm a veteran of the federal courts as well. Do you have proof that it crossed state lines?"

"It came from a pharmacist in Florida, my brother-in-law, since I was told it was needed for a chemical project and it was not available in Shelter Rock. So, I accommodated what I thought was a simple request. There were some emails back and forth."

"Did you pay for this chemical, Father?"

"No. It was sent gratis, so naturally I didn't charge the third party for it. It was a chemical called thallium."

"If I understand correctly," Polk said, "you passed this thallium along but never knew it was a poison?"

"It seems to have numerous uses. I Googled a few days ago and found that out."

"So, walk me through your timeline."

"I knew that Eric Robbins, owner of the Clarion, had become ill, but I never connected it to the donuts. Or poison. Even when he was hospitalized. I had no reason to. And then a penitent, in a moment of truth, blurted out to me during confession that he… or she… had poisoned… done the poisoning. I'm still not sure how."

"Thus, it's a confessional secret," Polk said. "But we'll go about this in a way that won't violate that sanctity. I think I already see the way out. You say this thallium has numerous uses?"

"Yes."

"Well, in this modern world, we can research on the spot. Let's take a look."

Polk opened his laptop and sat silent for several minutes tapping the keys. Then he closed the computer and said, "I've got the picture. And since thallium can go through the mails, I don't believe there is a federal issue. It's no different from mailing toothpaste. Let's go to work and end this disaster. We're in luck, because Susan Robertson is a very good and sympathetic judge."

Forty-one

It was a quarter past four when the case was called, and the courtroom was deserted except for two court officers, the stenographer, Sheriff Melendez, prosecutor Norcross and the judge's clerk. Judge Robertson was a tall, stately woman around fifty with brown hair, dark brown eyes and just a hint of lipstick.

"People of the State of Kansas versus Edvard Hoffmann," the clerk said.

"We waive the reading of the information," Roger Polk said.

"Mr. Polk," Judge Robertson said, "haven't seen you in some time. How are you?"

"Very well, Your Honor."

"What do we have here?" the judge asked. "These are very serious charges, Mr. Polk, and I understand that your client is a priest."

"What we have," Polk said, "is a horrendous case of mistaken identity."

"We have a man, no less a man who is a priest..." Norcross interjected, "...who tried to kill a citizen, a man who is one of his parishioners, by giving him a gift of donuts that were in fact poisoned. The victim was a man who had been very critical of the church on numerous occasions through the victim's newspaper."

"Pure conjecture, Your Honor. And as usual," Polk replied, "Mr. Norcross is fashioning a noose before the facts are even heard. Or in fact, before the arraignment has taken place. Perhaps we should have a conference where this matter can be cleared up in short order."

Norcross bristled. Sheriff Melendez stepped forward and said, "I think I can help clear this up, Your Honor, because I've been investigating. What Mr. Polk said is factually correct."

"But you signed the charging document," Judge Robertson said, shaking her head. "If nothing else, I am now totally confused. I think a conference, as unusual as it is before arraignment, is certainly warranted."

With that, she walked back into her chambers followed by an entourage. Roger Polk turned to Father Hoffmann and said, "You're not included at this point, Father, so wait here, please."

Father Hoffmann, bewildered, remained in the courtroom.

* * *

Judge Robertson gestured for Roger Polk and Nigel Norcross to take seats in the chairs facing her oak desk, which was piled high with files. The judge's clerk stood behind the judge as she removed her robe and hung it on the coat rack. A stenographer took a chair to the right of the desk, and the sheriff and the other court officer stood in the back of the room.

"Sheriff Melendez," Judge Robertson said, "before we get started, perhaps you can explain this confusion."

"I think I can, Your Honor," the sheriff said, stepping forward. "Mr. Robbins, the publisher of the Clarion, who is the victim here—the man who was poisoned, or I should say one of the two men who were poisoned—recently lost his mother, after the paper was—"

"I think we're all aware of what happened at the Clarion," the judge said. "It brought the attention of the entire nation, unfortunately, to Shelter Rock, and to this county, to the embarrassment of the entire legal community here."

The sheriff continued. "Father Hoffmann, as part of his clerical routine, regularly visits parishioners and also members of the community in time of need. He was given a poison called thallium by a third party, which Father Hoffmann received by mail from a relative out of state, and which he obtained as a favor for that third party. He was also given donuts by that third party with specific instructions to give them to Mr. Robbins at the newspaper. Father Hoffmann did so, and it turns out that the donuts contained that poison."

Nigel Norcross interrupted. "If he got the poison by mail out of state, then we're talking about a federal crime, and this case has to go to the federal court in Wichita before we even get started."

Roger Polk shook his head and raised a hand. "Nigel, can you just listen to the sheriff before you build the gallows, for God's sake?"

"That would be a good idea," Judge Robertson said. "Sheriff, please continue."

Sheriff Melendez said, "Thallium is a poison with several uses. It's deadly when ingested, but perfectly legal to be shipped by mail. So much for the federal aspect of the case. The Father received it and gave it to the parishioner who had requested it, thinking it was for some chemical project, completely ignorant of the fact that it was intended to be used as a poison.

"Father Hoffmann then passed the donuts poisoned with thallium to Mr. Robbins, thinking it was a benevolent gift, not a poison. When the donuts were consumed, Mr. Robbins got violently ill, actually close to death, and was rushed to the hospital. At this point, Atticus Duvall, who was visiting Eric, was also sickened when he ate part of one of the donuts. Someone else suggested it might be thallium. This proved correct, and an antidote was obtained from a hospital in Kansas City. I am happy to say that Mr. Robbins is on the way to recovery. Which does not excuse the criminal intent of the real perpetrator."

"Then what led you to file this charge against the priest?" Judge Robertson asked.

"Before my investigation was complete, Mr. Norcross, the prosecutor, wanted to move immediately, so I had no choice but to file the criminal information," Sheriff Melendez said.

"But if the priest is innocent, why didn't you say so?" Norcross asked.

"You preempted him all by yourself, Nigel," Polk said, "with your usual rush to judgment."

"Gentlemen," Judge Robertson said. "Sheriff, please continue."

"Father Hoffmann disclosed to me that the actual perpetrator confessed to him," the sheriff said, "but he did so during a confessional, and what is disclosed in confession cannot be shared by a priest—even if it means the priest goes to jail when he is innocent. This is the reason we are here. Anyway, I continued to pursue the case without any disclosure by Father Hoffmann, and without him breaking the sacred seal of the confessional. I have concluded that investigation just this morning and stand ready to arrest the actual perpetrator."

"And are you ready to put all this on the record?" the judge asked.

"I am ready to withdraw the complaint and effect an arrest," Sheriff Melendez said.

"I feel like a fool," Nigel Norcross said.

"If the shoe fits," Roger Polk said.

They adjourned to the courtroom, and the complaint was withdrawn.

Outside the courtroom, Father Hoffmann said, "Sheriff, I am forever in your debt. But how did you accomplish this without me disclosing the penitent?"

"I still haven't made the arrest yet, so let's leave it there at the moment."

With tears in his eyes, Father Hoffmann shook the hand of Roger Polk so strenuously that Polk had to pull his hand away. "I can't thank you enough," he said, "and we never discussed a fee, but please send me your bill. It saved my life. And my career in the church. Literally."

"Your thanks should be to the sheriff," Polk said. "He's really the one who was able to solve the case without violating the confession. As to a fee, this one is on me. With my blessings, if you will."

"If anything," Father Hoffmann said, "this entire incident only fortifies my faith and makes me realize how important it is in my life. God was literally looking down."

Forty-two

The following afternoon, the *Clarion* was advised there would be a press conference at the sheriff's office at four o'clock. Eric Robbins was still not well enough to attend, so Natalie Dawner, one of his reporters, attended in his place. So did Atticus, accompanied by Alison.

The sheriff, looking very somber, faced the small contingent, including a string reporter from the Associated Press. He announced, "At this time, I announce the arrest of Mayor David Fielder of Shelter Rock on the charge of attempted murder, assault with intent to do grievous bodily harm, and attempted manslaughter by means of poisoning another human being. I have copies of the information available here and will take a few questions."

He handed out copies of the indictment. Natalie Dawner, who was used to handling legal notices and societal information, appeared perplexed. Alison raised her hand.

"Yes?" Sheriff Melendez said. "And you are?"

"Alison Powers of the Washington Post, here on behalf of the Shelter Rock Clarion."

All eyes fixed on Alison, who said, "Sheriff, can you give us a little background on these very serious charges?"

The sheriff launched into a recitation of the facts, much as he had done the previous day in the chambers of Judge Robertson. His explanation included the fact that Father Hoffmann had not disclosed the name of the perpetrator.

Alison asked, "Then how were you able to determine that the mayor allegedly had committed these crimes?"

"Good question," the sheriff said. "Our investigation led us to the shipment of the chemical substance, called thallium, which Father Hoffmann had disclosed without breaching the confidentiality of the confession. The shipment was sent by the priest's brother-in-law in Florida. We contacted the brother-in-law, a pharmacist, and he confirmed that he had shipped it to Father Hoffmann. Then, Jennie Smith, an employee of the church as well as a parishioner, advised us that Father Hoffmann frequently started his rounds at Fielder's Foods, of which David Fielder is the proprietor. We also learned that it was not unusual for Father Hoffmann to present gifts of food or candies to people he visited.

"There is a history of bad blood between the mayor and the Clarion. When confronted by us with this information, Mr. Fielder acknowledged his conduct, although claiming he never intended to commit homicide but just wanted to punish the Clarion for what he perceived as a long series of editorial abuses and to teach a lesson. Unfortunately for him, it went way beyond what was intended and resulted in almost fatal results. After being read his rights, Mayor Fielder made a full confession, which was recorded. He is currently in custody and will be arraigned in district court tomorrow."

* * *

Mayor Fielder appeared with an attorney in district court and was released after posting bail of one hundred thousand dollars. Prosecutor Norcross had requested bail of one million dollars because of the attempted murder charge, but Judge Robertson fixed it at a lower amount because of Fielder's standing in the community, his local roots, and after his pledge to abide by any directive of the court. Fielder's attorney assured him that since he had no criminal past, and only sought to punish Eric Robbins and not kill him, that a fair resolution could be worked out with the court.

Mayor Fielder called an emergency meeting of the city council for that evening, and the members were shocked when they learned of the charges. Fielder immediately took a leave of absence and was replaced by Jeannette O'Connor, a member of the council, as acting mayor.

Eric Robbins was still at home, recovering from the poisoning. When he was brought up to date on Fielder's charges, he asked Alison to write the story for the current week's edition of the *Clarion,* which was due out on Friday. She hesitated, but after conferring with Mort, agreed to write the article without a byline so as not to impinge on her employment with the *Post.* The paper printed an extra five hundred copies of the weekly edition, and as word spread through the county, all copies were quickly gobbled up.

* * *

On Saturday, Father Hoffmann called Tish Duvall and said, "We have to talk."

She responded, "Yes, darling, we certainly do. I understand now why you couldn't make any disclosure to me, and I was so wrong. *So* wrong. How soon can we get together again and go on from here?"

They arranged to meet at the church that evening and drive to the reservoir where they could talk privately. She picked him up—he was not in his clerical garb—and they traveled halfway to the reservoir on 190th Street, pulling off the highway at an observation spot. They got out and sat on a bench. There was virtually no passing traffic.

Tish reached out for his hand, which he pulled away. Tish looked down at her own extended arm, pulled it back, and said, "Where to start? This has been a horrible week, the worst week of my life. First, that terrible woman and the scene at the council meeting. How could we have been so careless, and where was she creeping around and spying on us? And then those charges against you, and the fact that I misunderstood the whole thing. Thank God, it's behind us, and now we can go on with our lives. We have so much to look forward to."

"That's part of what we have to discuss," Father Hoffmann said. "I think the first thing we have to do is reassess our lives. God has been very gracious to me, and it is because of divine intervention that I sit here with you tonight."

A somber look darkened Tish's face. "Reassess? I don't understand."

"I realize that the Church is too important for me to just walk away."

"You don't have to walk away. You can still be just as religious as you want, but not be a priest. You can resign the priesthood and become a deacon. Still a leader in the Church. We can be together. We'll just move away. I give up my tenure, and you give up your pulpit. But we'll have each other."

She reached out and clasped him tightly in her arms.

He did not pull away. "It's deeper than that, love," Father Hoffmann said. "You are and have been my love. I hope you understand that."

"Deeper… What does that mean? Deeper how?"

"I can't leave the Church. I cannot leave the priesthood. God has intervened in my life, and I realize now that this truly is my calling. I think I knew it all along but was too weak to admit it."

Exasperated, Tish said, "Weak? Weak when you were all over me? Weak when you sucked my tits and fingered… you know what… when you entered me? We fucked. Plain and simple, Ed—we fucked! Those groans of pleasure were not from God, they were from *you*!" Her voice and her temperature were rising simultaneously, and even though they were alone, he glanced around to make certain no one was near.

"We have sinned, both of us," Father Hoffmann said. "Contrition and penance are required to cleanse our souls. In a few days, I am going to see the bishop in Wichita and make a full confession. I made the appointment today."

"The bishop? Confession? You know what you are? You are a bastard! A son of a bishop, not a son of God. You take from me and then think you can just wash it away with a few prayers? You have destroyed my life!"

Tish was now screaming. She slapped him forcefully across the face.

He pulled his head back and rubbed his cheek in disbelief.

"You took my life!" Tish yelled. "You think I used birth control? I didn't. I wanted to get pregnant with your baby. What's your bishop going to say to that?"

"You're pregnant?"

"I might be. And if I am, what do you say about that, you hypocritical bastard?"

Tish jumped to her feet, and as he started to get up, she pushed him hard in the chest. He fell backward over the bench, and she headed for her car.

"Tish," Father Hoffmann cried out, "you don't understand. The Church is my life. I transgressed, we both sinned, but God can make it right." He got to his feet and ran after her.

As she started up the engine, she said, "Tell God to get you back to Shelter Rock." She spat the words like bullets. The tears were rolling down her face, and she choked as she sobbed. "Cry to your damned bishop and let him pat you on the head and do your penance. And then what?"

"Be reasonable," he pleaded. "No one can take away what we had. We will always have that. The bishop will understand. He's a very progressive and understanding man, and we can always be friends. I'll do my penance, and then I'll get another congregation somewhere else. I can start over. And so can you!"

"You know what you can do?" Tish screamed. "You can go fuck yourself!"

With that, she pulled away, spraying dirt and pebbles. Tish headed toward Hillsboro, and Father Hoffmann stood at the side of the road looking back toward Shelter Rock. He crossed the road and started slowly walking back to the church.

Tish drove, sobbing and wailing, almost hysterical. She had no destination in mind at first, but just drove, muttering, "A bastard. They're all bastards. Every one of them. They take from you and then break your heart."

Then she decided to continue on to the reservoir, their original destination.

Forty-three

In Atticus's condo, the two couples had a discussion at dinner. Mort and Danni wanted to get home to the twins, Mort needed to get back to work at the *Post,* and Alison agreed to join them, although she wanted to spend a few more days with Atticus. Atticus offered to fly them to Kansas City in the morning. Mort said they'd leave early enough for him to turn in the car they had rented. Reservations would be no problem.

"I'm up for the flight," Alison said, touching Atticus on his arm.

He smiled. "But we've still got tonight," he said, "so let's make it special. The county fair is in Hillsboro, and that's always a treat."

"A real county fair?" Danni said. "A Ferris wheel? I haven't been on one of those since I was a kid. It was in the Rockaways, on Long Island."

"Ferris wheels, merry-go-rounds, crazy cars, booths, exhibitions… the works," Atticus said.

Mort said, "Heights are not for me. I'll stay grounded, if it's all the same."

"I'm with you," Alison said, gesturing to Mort.

Danni said, "Party poopers."

They drove east on 190th Street toward Hillsboro with Mort driving the rental car. About halfway to Hillsboro, which was only ten miles away, they passed an observation spot and Atticus said, "That looked like Tish's car back there. Wonder what she's doing out here?"

Alison directed Mort, "Just keep driving."

They parked in the fair's parking area—to Mort's surprise, parking was free—and entered the grounds after paying a nominal admission fee. There were booths set up for exhibitors—artists with their paintings, handcrafted jewelry, a variety of ready-to-wear items, and a wide variety of food choices. The grounds were crowded, and it was clear that people had come from far and wide to enjoy the annual event.

Danni and Atticus immediately opted for the Ferris wheel, while Mort and Alison wandered the grounds, stopping in at the various booths but not making any purchases.

* * *

On her way to the reservoir, Tish drove recklessly, sobbing and retching, trying to compose herself. She had just seen her life's plans destroyed. All of her emotions came back to her. But as she passed the fairgrounds, on an impulse, she decided to stop. Without giving it much thought, except to perhaps cheer herself up, she parked and prepared to enter the grounds. After wiping her eyes in the rearview mirror with a tissue and staring for a long moment at her reflection, she dug into her purse, took out and applied some blush, and got out of the car. She was still breathing hard from crying and thought that maybe a new piece of jewelry would cheer her up.

* * *

Danni and Atticus rejoined the others after their ride, and they continued walking around the booths and the exhibits.

"Hey, Mr. Duvall," came a shout. "Come and sign our petition."

Three high school students stood at a table proclaiming "Sign the book-banning petition. Your freedom is at stake."

Atticus looked at the trio in surprise. "Bonnie, Jeff, Marisa—what are you guys doing here?"

He turned to his companions and said, "These kids were all students of mine. Now they're in the high school. I'm surprised you remember me," he said to the students.

"Aw, come on," Marisa said. "We never forget our favorite teachers. You were the best."

Jeff, a sandy haired six-footer in jeans, said, "We heard what they're trying to do—banning books from the library—so we thought this was a great spot to talk to people and get them to sign our petition to stop it."

"We got over three hundred signatures already," Bonnie said. "And we've only been here since noon."

"Can out of towners sign?" Mort asked.

"Anybody that cares," Jeff said, thrusting a pen at Mort.

He bent over, signed the petition and handed the pen to Danni, who followed and handed the pen to Alison, who also signed.

Atticus said, "I think this is great that you kids would take part of your summer to engage in an exercise like this."

"It's not an exercise," Bonnie said. "We've got half the senior class involved in this. We're taking turns on different days and at different times. We don't want them taking our books off the shelves and making decisions about what's appropriate for our suggestible minds. We want to make our own decisions on what to read."

Atticus stepped forward and took the pen from Alison, bent over, and was about to sign when a voice interrupted.

"Go ahead and sign!" Tish said. She was standing behind the teens. "The school board would love to have a chance to terminate you." Her hair was disheveled, her eyes red, her tone harsh. They all spun around to face her.

"We're not doing anything wrong," Bonnie said, thrusting out her chin, "except exercising our rights. Besides, you have no jurisdiction over us. We're in high school."

This was the culmination of a really bad day for Tish. She probably should have ignored the fair and gone on to the reservoir to contemplate the disaster of her life. Instead, she gave a roar and rushed the students, turning the table over on Marisa, who valiantly tried to save the materials from scattering. The table and Marisa crashed to the ground, and a crowd started to gather, attracted by the turmoil.

"There's your jurisdiction," Tish shouted, "and you're probably violating rules by doing something political on the fairgrounds. We'll see about that."

"I'll bet that the First Amendment is someplace in your schoolbooks," Danni said, stepping forward. "Although, on second thought, you've probably banned the Bill of Rights as well. Politicians use fairgrounds all the time to campaign. These kids are just exercising their rights. Why don't you take a hike or get back on your broom."

About a dozen feet separated the two women, and Tish roared, "I've had enough of you and your Eastern bullshit." With fists clenched, she rushed at Danni, who stood motionless until Tish was about four feet away. Suddenly, Danni raised her right arm straight from the shoulder, fist closed. Tish crashed into it face first and went down, spurting blood from her nose.

Tish rolled around on the ground, getting covered with dust, holding her nose and screaming, "I'll have your ass!"

A security guard, attracted by the noise, rushed over. He was a stocky young man in his thirties, wearing jeans and a too-large blue shirt with a badge pinned to it. He had a pistol on his hip—not the law enforcement type of weapon like a Glock, but a revolver in a loose holster. He went to help Tish to her feet, and as he bent over, she grabbed the pistol and swung it toward Danni.

Mort pushed Danni out of the line of fire, sending her sprawling, and faced Tish. Atticus grabbed Mort and pushed him aside just as Tish fired. The report of the pistol was loud as it reverberated through the fairgrounds. People ducked for cover or ran away screaming. It was chaos.

"Shooter!" the guard shouted, as Tish stared at the barrel of the pistol as if not comprehending what she had done. Atticus clutched his side, blood seeping through his fingers, and fell to the ground. Alison ran to him.

Mort stepped forward and kicked at Tish's wrist, but she turned at the last second and he struck her in the back. She was still clutching the pistol as she went sprawling to the ground again. Mort bellowed, "Call 911."

Tish's eyes glistened, as she muttered, "My life. It's over." Then she ran off still clutching the pistol.

Atticus screamed at her as she ran, clutching his side, "Tish! Stop! For God's sake, stop!"

Tish ran about fifty yards to the Ferris wheel and screamed at the attendant, "Take me up!"

"Lady, you need a ticket," the attendant said, until she pushed the pistol into his face.

"Take me up," she demanded.

"Okay, okay."

There were a few patrons dangling from the chairs on the Ferris wheel, which had been stopped for people to get off. Tish threw herself into a seat, and the attendant started the wheel's motion. People already on the Ferris wheel, unaware of what had just transpired, looked on in confusion.

The Ferris wheel began its slow revolution. As Tish's chair reached its highest point about eighty feet in the air, the chair was swinging back and forth, back and forth. She was not strapped in and suddenly stood up. The seat tilted precariously. Suddenly, the gun flew out of her hand and crashed to the ground as she leaned over and either jumped or fell, her body smashing to the ground. A pool of blood immediately started forming around her body.

Forty-four

Hillsboro Community Hospital was only two miles from the county fairgrounds, and an emergency EMT team arrived by ambulance within two minutes of the 911 call, made by one of the bystanders. Atticus was holding his side as blood seeped through his fingers, but the initial diagnosis by EMTs was that Tish's bullet had entered and exited his side without damaging any organs. A flesh wound.

Police arrived within moments of the ambulance, and one officer was questioning Danni and Mort while his partner inspected Tish's body. The EMTs had already confirmed that she was dead, although there was never any doubt. Her last moments must have been pure terror as she plunged to the ground.

Her body was then covered with a tarp awaiting the medical examiner, and one police car with a sergeant followed the ambulance to the hospital. The other two officers, joined by two more about ten minutes later, started taking statements from witnesses, including Danni and Mort, the high school students, the Ferris wheel attendant, and those bystanders who had been witnesses. The stories were very consistent, which is not always the case at a traumatic event like a violent death. A photographer was taking pictures, although he appeared to be a civilian and not a police officer, but they all seemed to know each other.

Hillsboro Community Hospital was a modern facility, and as Atticus was rushed in through the emergency room entrance, he was jabbering almost incoherently. "Tish is gone. I can't believe it.

She was so much a part of my life for years, and now she's dead. Just like that. Tonight was so out of character for her. She never acts like that. She was always measured and deliberate, and I can't reconcile her conduct tonight with her personality. It just doesn't make sense. What was she even doing at the fair? And did you see her when she arrived? Her makeup was smeared. She was really pissed about something for sure. The kids just set it off. It doesn't make sense."

The medical staff cleaned the wound and gave Atticus a tetanus shot and an antibiotic. The doctor, a young Asian man, wanted him to stay overnight for observation, particularly because of the trauma he had just endured, but he insisted on going home to Shelter Rock.

The preliminary police investigation determined that an angry Tish had arrived where the students were petitioning, flew into an unexplained rage and upended their table while berating them. Danni had stepped forward to defend the students, which further enraged Tish and she charged Danni with fists raised, only to be cold cocked at the last second by Danni's straight-arm fist. The security officer then arrived. Tish grabbed his pistol and appeared ready to shoot at Danni. Mort shoved her away and Tish aimed at Mort, who had not even been involved in the confrontation. Mort, in turn, was shoved aside by Atticus, who took the bullet.

All the statements were consistent, but no one could explain Tish's belligerent frame of mind from the outset. After the police took preliminary statements, the crowd began to disperse. Danni and Mort were given directions to the hospital.

At the hospital, the police sergeant asked them to come in the following day to formalize their statements, and Mort explained that they were heading back to DC, showed his press credentials, and arranged for the statements to be faxed or emailed. What would forever remain unexplained was what had precipitated Tish Duvall's behavior that evening.

They all got back to Atticus's condo at about three in the morning. Atticus was with them, insisting that he could treat his minor wound at home instead of spending time in the hospital.

Not knowing any of the events at the fairground until the next day, Father Hoffmann trudged about a mile before a car heading for Shelter Rock took pity on the hitchhiker and gave him a ride back to his rectory. No one, except the medical examiner and her assistant, would ever know that the autopsy of Tish Duvall showed she was two months pregnant, something even the dead woman didn't know for sure.

* * *

Danni and Mort left as planned the following morning, but Alison said she was staying an additional day or two until she was sure Atticus was okay. The story that appeared in the *Clarion* on Friday spoke of the "tragic death of Shelter Rock school's administrator Tish Duvall in a fall from the Ferris wheel at the county fair." It did not mention any of the events that had preceded her fall.

* * *

Upon his return to the *Post*, Mort was visited in his office by managing editor Marcie Gold.

"You know I'm a pretty liberal person," Marcie said, "but your job is here in DC. Especially now that all the information you need for a Sunday follow-up opinion piece on book banning is complete. You can't keep running back and forth to the Midwest. And as for Alison, well, I'm under a lot of pressure because we're cutting down personnel in the newsroom by 20 percent, and she doesn't have your standing or personal time to justify keeping her."

"You can't let her go," Mort pleaded. "Especially after that great series on censorship. And she'll be back in a day or two. We just had some unexpected tragedies out there two days ago, and her fiancé—or whatever he is—was shot by his ex-wife."

"I don't believe it," Marcie said. "You were involved in another shooting? I need a Valium."

"No, not me," Mort said. "I mean, this deranged woman was going to shoot me, but Alison's boyfriend pushed me out of the way and took the bullet."

217

Marcie put a hand to her forehead and groped for one of Mort's chairs. "Lay this one on me, but gently, please," Marcie said.

"We were at the county fair—" Mort said.

Marcie interrupted. "Hold on. I thought you all went out there because that local editor and Alison's boyfriend suddenly got very ill."

"Not just ill. They were poisoned."

"Poisoned?" Marcie said. "Who the hell poisoned them?"

"We thought it was the priest, because he's the one who brought the tainted donuts."

"Wait—a priest poisoned the editor? Why haven't I seen an article about this from you or Alison? You are journalists still, no?"

"It wasn't the priest, though," Mort said. "It was the mayor."

Marcie gasped. "Make that a *bottle* of Valium. The mayor poisoned the editor of the paper? And you still had time to go to the county fair?"

Mort gave a sheepish look. "Actually, it was Danni who actually figured it out—about the poison, that is. And everyone is recovering." Mort paused, and exclaimed, "Oh, my God, they're going to have to exhume Margery!"

"Exhume?" Marcie said. "Margery? Who's Margery, and why do they have to exhume her?" Marcie brought both hands to her face and covered her eyes.

"I've got to call the sheriff out there," Mort said. "How did I overlook that?"

"The sheriff? You're involved with the sheriff too? Mort, I don't know how I can absorb much more of your adventures without a good therapist."

Mort smiled. "I can give you the number for my shrink. He's really good. Or do you think that would be a conflict of interest?" He paused. "Look, I can simplify the whole thing."

"Please," Marcie said. "I'm begging you."

"We went out there because Eric—he's the local editor— was getting terribly sick, and then Atticus—he's Alison's fiancé, or significant other, or whatever—got the same symptoms and their hair started falling out."

"Their hair fell out?" Marcie said in disbelief.

"Margery was the publisher of the Clarion—the newspaper that ran the censorship stories Alison wrote about. The phony police raid. You know."

Marcie nodded.

Mort said, "She was ninety-eight. Died the day after the search, and everyone assumed it was the stress. But if Eric and Atticus were poisoned, maybe she was too, and they better check that out to add to the charges if it's true. So, they're going to have to exhume her.

"Anyway, Danni said the poison was thallium—and it was—so we flew to Kansas City for the antidote. And all was copacetic. Then, at the city council meeting, Danni got into a fracas with Tish… that's Atticus's ex-wife—about banning books in the school."

"Thank God," Marcie said. "Something relevant at last."

"And Danni kicked her ass with Robert's Rules of Order. Her attempt to involve the city council in the book ban fell flat, and then this lady stood up in the audience and accused her—Tish, that is, Atticus's ex—of being naked in the church and having an affair with the priest."

"With the priest?" Marcie said. "The poisoner? He was having an affair with this woman?"

"We never proved anything, because she denied it, and then she died on the Ferris wheel."

At this point, Marcie couldn't even speak.

"Well, she either fell or jumped," Mort said. "Made an ungodly mess."

Marcie blanched. "And the priest?" she said.

"No one ever got a chance to talk to him about the relationship, at least by the time we left," Mort said. "But they were apparently pretty tight. So, two nights ago, before we were scheduled to come home, Atticus suggested we should go to the county fair. And we were all in, because of the stressful few days. We went."

"And?"

"And Tish showed up, in an ugly mood, and she turned over the table that the high school kids were using to sign petitions against book banning—"

"Ah, book banning. Something of relevance again," Marcie interrupted.

"And Danni confronted her for being a dork and going bullshit at the student—a nice group of high school seniors. And she was already pissed at Danni because of the city council, so she came running at Danni, ready to fight, and Danni just raised her fist and Tish's face ran into it and she went down."

"Good old Danni," Marcie said, with a tone of sarcasm.

"Next thing you know, Tish grabbed the gun from a security guard—she was enraged—and was going to shoot Danni, and I pushed her out of the way. So Tish turned on me, and Atticus pushed me out of the way as she fired, and he took the bullet. Only a flesh wound, but he probably saved my life."

"You really ought to turn this into a six-part HBO series," Marcie said. "I think I understand now, maybe, but do you think you can put this whole thing behind you and do a Sunday follow-up feature on book banning? About two thousand words. That is what we're paying you for. Play with it, and I'll see what I can do about saving Alison."

"As soon as I call the sheriff," Mort said, "and find out whether Margery was also poisoned."

Forty-five

A Week later, Mort returned home from the *Post* at five-thirty, earlier than usual, in time to help feed the twins and have dinner with Danni.

"A little quality time with my gorgeous wife and those great twins she presented me with," Mort said, leaning down and petting Katie, whose tail was working overtime. He leaned over and grabbed a treat from the bowl on the counter. She devoured it ravenously.

Before he had a chance to say anything else, Danni said, "Alison called. She and Atticus want to have a Zoom call with us tonight. I set it up for eight o'clock."

"You know, she's a great writer, and I'm really fond of her, but she's pushed the envelope so far at the office that I can't keep sticking my neck out. She's out of vacation time, out of personal time, and really, almost out of job time."

"That would be a pity, but I think that's one of the things she wanted to talk about."

"Uh oh," Mort said. "That sounds ominous."

At eight, Danni and Mort were seated in front of her computer, waiting to connect. Promptly, Alison and Atticus appeared on the screen.

"Atticus has questions for Danni," Alison said, "and then I want to talk with Mort."

"Fire away," Danni said.

"First, how are you guys?" Atticus asked.

"Hanging in," Mort said, unemotionally.

"Don't listen to Mr. Downer," Danni said, pushing her way in front of Mort. "We're fine, the twins are fine, already down for the night, Mort is working on a big Sunday follow-up feature on book banning for the opinion section, and I feel that I'm just about ready to tackle the next semester and take a shot at constitutional law. And how are you? Is the wound healing?"

"All going well. How are you at real estate?" Atticus asked.

"Not a specialty, but go ahead."

"It turns out that when Tish and I got divorced, we never did anything about title to the house—our house, which we agreed to at the time. Kansas is a no-fault divorce state, and we knew that things between us were over, so we got some forms online, filled them out and went to Wichita. Presto, we were divorced. Irreconcilable differences, which was definitely the case. We agreed she'd take the house, and I'd find a place to live. No alimony from me. She was making more than me, anyway. We each had our own IRAs, which made it pretty simple. I had some money from my military days, but she wanted no part of it. And things went on that way for over two years until she died at the fairgrounds. The question is the house. What happens to the house?"

"When you divorced, did you sign any papers regarding the house?"

"We didn't sign anything except the divorce papers. It was plain and simple."

"Pretty simple," Danni said, "but not really so simple under those circumstances. You owned the house by what is called 'tenants by the entireties,' which applies to married couples. When you divorced, you became joint tenants, with rights of survivorship. In effect, you gave her your half of the house at the divorce, but you never terminated the joint tenancy. Did she have a will?"

"No will," Atticus said. "She was an only child and her parents were dead."

"Well, my friend," Danni said, "it looks like you just became the owner of a house."

"Just like that?" Atticus said.

"That's how the law works. You both should have had wills. On her death, without anything else intervening legally, you are the other joint tenant and title passes to you—divorce or not."

"I still don't have a will," Atticus said. "We were a young couple. Nobody ever thinks of dying young."

"Well, you just learned a lesson. You're going to need a local lawyer, someone who knows real estate, to correct the title. It probably can be done without an estate proceeding, just using the death certificate. Then, you should sit down and get yourself a will."

"I know a guy like that right here. Good attorney named Jeff Grant. Specializes in real estate. Straight shooter. As to the will, that's something I will take care of with my last wife."

"You were married once before?" Danni asked, surprised.

Atticus and Alison broke into broad smiles on the Zoom. "No," he said, "but Alison and I have been talking marriage. And she will definitely be my last wife."

"Congratulations!" Mort and Danni said simultaneously.

"But I don't want to live in that house," Alison chimed in. "Comes with too many bad memories."

"From what I read, it's a sellers' market," Danni said, "so you should have no problem in that regard, once you get everything settled."

"If I might butt in," Mort said. "What is Alison, the almost newlywed, going to do about her job here in Washington?"

"That's the other thing we wanted to talk about," Alison said. "I'm not coming back to Washington, Mort, except maybe to pack up my things and dispose of my apartment."

"You're going to commute?" Mort asked. "From Kansas to DC?"

"No, that's the other thing," Alison said. "We've been talking with Eric, who's now back at the Clarion, and his brush with death made him realize how short life really is. He doesn't want to die in the saddle, like his mother. He'd like to stay on as publisher and make me the editor. I just accepted his offer. So, I'll get some western jeans and cowboy boots and become a Midwesterner." She paused. "I mean, you guys have been great, and that goes for Marcie and everyone at the Post, but Atticus made me an offer that I just can't refuse."

Atticus said, "And we want you guys to be Best Man and Matron of Honor. We've all been down a very long road in a short period of time."

"You can say that again," Mort said.

"We've all been down a very long road in a short period of time," Atticus repeated, and they all laughed.

"Have you set a date?" Danni asked.

Alison replied, "This is all very sudden… and no, not yet. There are so many things to tie up."

"Do your families know?" Mort asked.

"Yes," Alison said. "My folks are thrilled. And I'll be closer to them in Louisiana. Mom has been dying to have grandchildren."

"I only have my mother," Atticus said, "and she never cared for Tish to begin with. She'll love Alison."

"Well, since you don't have a date, I'll float an idea," Danni said. "It would mean you and your families coming to Washington, DC, over Labor Day, to be married by J.J. Richter, my father-in-law, the senior US Supreme Court Justice. If we can work out all the coordinates at his annual Labor Day bash. He did a great job for us, and that would really spice up the day."

"You just blew my mind," Atticus said. They spoke for a few minutes longer and agreed to Zoom again in a few days.

Forty-six

Melbourne, Florida

Meredith Bigote was not expecting company when her doorbell rang. In the traumatic few weeks since her interview with Mort, her visit by her brother, and the exposure of her three-way affair, her membership with Families for Freedom had been terminated, and she had been held up to ridicule and embarrassment among her friends, her church and even her children. She avoided going out of the house and got nervous every time the doorbell rang, fearing that it was somehow connected to her transgressions with her best friend and her husband. Chelsea's husband had seen to it that their sordid affair had resulted in much unwanted attention.

Meredith was shocked to see her brother, Edvard Hoffmann, the priest, towering over her at the door. She noticed his car parked at the curb.

"Ed! What are you doing here? No notice. Everything okay?"

"No, not okay. In fact, a lot of sadness and problems," Father Hoffmann said.

She invited him in, and they moved into the alcove in the kitchen. "What is it?" she asked after brewing a cup of coffee in the Keurig. He paused for about fifteen seconds, saying nothing. Then he spoke slowly. "I am on my way to the Saint Leo Sanctury House and the Abbey in Saint Leo."

"The Saint Leo Abbey? I know of it," Meredith said. "It's in the middle of nowhere. Practically in the Everglades. Why on earth...?"

"It's complicated, but I'll be there for at least the next six months. I just thought I'd stop here and see you first. I have all my things in the car."

"Your things?"

"I'm no longer with St. John's," he said, "and I'm no longer living in Kansas. Literally everything I own is in the trunk of the car. I want to leave a few items with you. In terms of material things, it's not much, which is fine, under the circumstances."

"Ed, you're frightening me," Meredith said. "What is it?"

"Going to St. Leo is the beginning of a penance as I attempt a Sacrament of Reconciliation, basically, to restore my soul. Somewhere along the way, I lost it," Father Hoffmann said.

"Reconciliation?" Meredith said, alarmed. "Penance? What have you done?"

"I've sinned, I've broken my vows, I've offended everything that I believed in, and I only pray that I get absolution and can return to the Church."

"You're scaring the hell out of me," Meredith said. "How did this happen?"

"It happened because I was weak," he said. "It happened because the temptations of the flesh overcame my sensibilities, and I offended God. And now I must make amends—for my own soul, if nothing else."

"Temptations of the flesh?" Meredith said. "You weren't involved with a child, were you? Oh, my God! You'll be excommunicated!"

"Meredith, you know me better than that. Of course not. I would never defile a child. No, but I am a man. I had a relationship, a sexual relationship with Tish Duvall."

"Tish? Our editor? The woman I wrote the article with? But she was so invested in you, with us—in Families for Freedom. It had become our life, our calling. Although I do recall you saying, months ago, that she was flirtatious. Did she seduce you?"

"She did nothing I wasn't a willing participant in. We even talked of my leaving the priesthood and making a life together."

"I need a drink," Meredith said. "And you know I'm not a drinker. But this is too much." She got up, left the room and returned a minute later with a bottle of bourbon. She went to the cabinet and took out a glass. Looking at her brother, she asked, "Join me?"

He shook his head.

"You say she didn't seduce you, but I know you too well," Meredith said. "And I know the tricks of a woman. I have no doubt that she seduced you. She should be punished for what she got you into."

"She's been punished, Meredith. She's dead."

"Dead?" Meredith closed her eyes and crossed herself. "How?"

"We had a very unfortunate confrontation," Father Hoffmann said. "Our relationship, which had been discreet, was exposed, and I realized, after being charged with a serious crime, that my transgressions only reinforced what I knew all along—that my calling was to God, and my love was the Church. With all my soul. Not that I didn't care for her deeply. I did. When I told her I couldn't leave my calling, she got hysterical, and the next day she was dead. Probably suicide."

"How were you charged with a crime? Having an affair is not criminal."

"I better start at the beginning," Father Hoffmann said. And he related the story of the poisoned donuts and the subsequent investigation that resulted in him being charged and then the mayor being charged. He described the scene at the city council, though he knew only what Tish and Mayor Fielder had told him.

He had gone to Wichita to see the bishop, an appointment he had made before Tish's death, and confessed the entire story. The bishop was shocked but compassionate and understanding. After expressing his contrition, the bishop then made arrangements for him to go to St. Leo for six months of prayer and solitude to seek God's forgiveness, after which he would return to Wichita. If absolution was granted, he could go on with a new life.

"And then what?" Meredith asked.

"And then it could be anything from excommunication, which the bishop said was not probable, to denial of absolution, to a ministerial job in a rectory somewhere, or eventually a return to the pulpit in a new location—which I will pray for."

"And this all started because of your suggestion that we take steps to purify the libraries of the schools, a wonderful idea, and your suggestion that we form Families for Freedom. How could something so beneficial have practically destroyed our life in this community and left us ostracized. Ed, our children are in therapy and looking at us in a different light. My friendship with my best friend is now over, and Larry is trying to sell the pharmacy so that we can move somewhere and start over. Good God, the damage we've done!" Meredith said.

"We learn from our transgressions," Father Hoffmann said, "and it's all part of God's plan, I believe. A plan to make us stronger and better human beings."

They talked for another hour. Her brother declined Meredith's offer to spend a few days with her and the family. Father Hoffmann wanted to get to St. Leo and begin his period of penance. They discussed whether she should tell the family and decided they would definitely not inform the children, who already had more than enough to deal with.

Meredith walked her brother to the door, and he left. As the door closed, she burst into tears and spent the rest of the day thinking about how their lives had changed in the past three years.

Forty-seven

Washington, DC

The executive committee of the *Washington Post* met on Wednesday morning at ten in the office of the Executive Editor Scott Coombs. Present were the four managing editors including Marcie Gold and an invited visitor—Mort Ahrens.

Coombs, an overpowering Black man who had been an All-American basketball player at Georgetown before he embarked on his journalism career, wore black slacks, a black turtleneck and black sockless loafers. "You know," Coombs said, looking at Mort, "we try to program these Sunday special features about two months ahead. But every time we think we have a fixed date for you, you seem to need more time. What can we figure, while trying to accommodate your dalliance?"

Marcie Gold started to speak, but Coombs held up his hand in a silencing gesture.

"You know that the interviews," Mort said, "that Alison and I completed almost a month ago, are in the can, and we did that three-day spread. But every time I try to put this thing to bed, another legislature someplace does something crazy that I have to include. And then I have to seek out another expert or a professor or even an author to say how crazy it is."

He paused to see if Coombs would hurry him up. With no signal, he continued.

"This week it was Utah, which banned thirteen titles by the likes of Judy Blume or Margaret Atwood, and then I have to chase them down for a response. It's never ending. I would say we should plan it for the Sunday before Labor Day, because most of these legislative lunatics are on vacation in August. I'll get it done one way or the other."

"Preferably one way," Coombs said, "and not the other. I want this to knock the proverbial socks off. What the hell have they got against Judy Blume?"

Mort answered, "This new law, and there have been a bunch of really crazy ones from the conservative areas, says that if a book is on the banned list from any three school districts, or two districts and five charter school districts—of which they have over forty—that it has to be removed from the shelves of every school in the state. It must be 'legally disposed of,' whatever that means, and may not be sold or distributed anywhere in the state because it probably contains 'pornographic or indecent' material."

"That's insane," said Coombs. "Haven't they heard of the First Amendment? That law will never stand. It's vague on its face, to say nothing that community standards in one district might differ from those in another."

"Welcome to the club," Mort said. "Then I have to go to the authors, or some expert in constitutional law, or PEN America, or the ACLU for a cogent response, and it keeps spiraling out of control."

"Well, let's firm up your completion by Labor Day. If necessary, we'll put some kind of a caution or disclaimer on the article that the cut-off day for crazy legislators is such and such a date. This should be a hell of an article. I smell Pulitzer, Ahrens."

"I think you're smelling my perspiration," Mort said, to a room-wide laugh.

* * *

Almost a week later, another Zoom call with Alison and Atticus had Mort and Danni sitting in front of their monitor. After the usual greetings, Mort said, "It's been several weeks now, but I assume you would have let me know if Margery was also poisoned. Yes?"

"I should have called you yesterday when the results came back," Atticus said, "but I knew we were scheduled for a call tonight. The answer is no. After all that trouble and the court order, the exhumation results were negative. Bad enough that the poor woman died from the trauma that the police chief and his thugs put her through. Then, Eric had to get a court order and have her exhumed. The sheriff was on his side, because of the possibility of an additional crime. So, they dug her up, the medical people did their thing, and then she had to be buried again."

"How terrible," Danni said.

Atticus replied, "Yes, what a mess. Bottom line, no sign of thallium in her system. I guess Mayor Fielder didn't dislike her as much as Eric, or maybe she didn't like donuts. It was a shame they had to dig her up and go to all that trouble, but at least we have the answer. Now, the poor woman is finally at rest. In any event, Fielder's case is proceeding in the circuit court here, and it looks like he won't be giving anyone donuts for a long time. In addition to that, Father Hoffmann is no longer at St. John's, although the facts of his leaving are murky. He just sort of vanished."

"The priest is gone?" Mort said. "Maybe there was something to what that woman said at the city council meeting."

"Whatever," Atticus said. "But Tish, as difficult as she was, got more than she deserved. And we'll never really know about her and the priest. Or whether she fell or jumped. It's still a huge void."

Danni chimed in. "On to more pleasant things. Are we on track for the wedding? It will make the usual Labor Day party, which is great to begin with, a spectacular event."

"Our families are both really excited," Alison said. "And I'm still in awe that the judge is willing to do it."

"He did a great job for us," Danni said. "And he doesn't take tips. We wrote our own vows. You might consider that as well."

"Under advisement," Atticus said. "I have to add that the stories in the Clarion have never been this good. Thanks to Alison."

"He's not objective," Alison said. "Mort, how's the feature coming?"

"It will be out the day before Labor Day, one way or the other, but I'm not certain where it will be placed, since we no longer publish the Outlook Magazine on Sundays. Maybe in the Style section."

"Looking forward to it."

Forty-eight

On the day before Labor Day, the *Washington Post* carried the following feature on its front page: "Book Banning, Censorship, and its Toll on the First Amendment," with a byline by Mort Ahrens. Under the title, it read:

Irene Diamond, thirty-eight years old, mother of two young children.

Molly Perkins, fifty-two years old, award-winning author and novelist.

Tish Duvall, forty-three years old, teacher and grammar school administrator.

What do these women have in common?

They're all from the Midwest or the South, and in one form or another, book-banning played a part in their lives—and their deaths.

Irene Diamond was a Mississippi attorney, retained (without fee) to defend a librarian who had checked out the book *The Catcher in the Rye* to a sixteen-year-old. The book had been widely used in both high schools and middle schools but was attacked by the student's mother (who admitted during trial that she had never read it) because it was on a list of books that should be banned according to "Families for Freedom," an activist organization she belonged to. She professed to be religious and law-abiding, and she quoted from the Bible during her testimony. After a trial, the jury brought back a "not guilty" plea in a half hour, and the librarian was exonerated. The mother, infuriated and embarrassed, later stabbed the lawyer to death and left a Bible on her body. The Bible was open to a passage she had quoted during her testimony.

Molly Perkins was the author of two award-winning novels and a widely respected writer who lived in Mississippi and decided to open a bookstore in Biloxi called "Banned-Aid." She intended to offer a wide variety of books from children's literature to all genres of fiction including, particularly, books that had been banned from schools throughout the state. On the night before her store was to officially open, she was murdered in an explosion that leveled the premises. A local fire official is currently being held and charged with her murder. The official's wife was active in the organization "Families for Freedom."

Tish Duvall was a respected grammar school administrator in Kansas, devoted to right wing and conservative causes. She was the editor of the monthly newsletter published by "Families for Freedom," which was circulated to its members all over the nation. (It has hundreds of chapters and boasts several hundred thousand members and is affiliated with several right wing political and conservative groups, including some with religious Christian agendas.) At the Kansas County Fair, she had a confrontation with a group of local high school seniors who had set up a booth opposing book banning and were soliciting signatures for a petition in that regard. The confrontation escalated into fisticuffs, she grabbed a pistol from a security guard, shot a bystander (who happened to be her ex-husband), commandeered the Ferris wheel at gunpoint, and either jumped or fell to her death from its highest point.

[Disclosure: She initially pointed the pistol at a woman who had stepped in to defend the rights of the students to petition, my wife, then at me (I was present at the fair and in Kansas gathering material for this article), but I was pushed out of the way by the man who was shot.]

While these are isolated events, there have been numerous other incidents of violence throughout the nation as a result of book banning efforts that will be discussed later in this article. Some have resulted in severe punishments, such as the case of Stella Hobbs, a grammar school teacher in Kansas who led her first-grade class in the singing of "Rainbow Connection." The song was made popular by Kermit the Frog on Sesame Street, the multiple-award-winning children's television show. Ms. Hobbs was in her first year on the job, but the school board determined that the song, which mentioned rainbows, was suggestive of an LGBTQ culture and fired her without a hearing. (Ms. Hobbs was neither gay nor bisexual.) That case is currently being litigated in the federal courts. She is being represented by the American Civil Liberties Union.

THE HISTORY OF BOOK BANNING

Book banning has existed as long as man has had the ability to write and as long as critics have had opinions about those writings. There has always been someone ready to question or object to the writings of others. In ancient Egypt, one can imagine a person tearing up or setting on fire something written on papyrus because he deemed it objectionable. In the eighteenth century, Voltaire (the nom de plume of Francois-Marie Arouet), a passionate advocate of both freedom of speech and religion, stated, "Think for yourselves and let others enjoy the privilege to do so, too."

In the Bill of Rights, ratified in 1791, the United States marked the importance of freedom of speech by adopting the First Amendment to the Constitution, providing "Congress shall make no law... abridging the freedom of speech, or of the press..." The majority of these attacks on freedom of speech thus passed to the states where there were as many different interpretations of the meaning of "free speech" as there were states.

One of the first books to be threatened throughout the United States was *Uncle Tom's Cabin* by Harriet Beecher Stowe, first published in 1851, because of its approach to slavery and its pro-abolitionist leanings. Many books, even textbooks or medical texts, have been deemed pornographic or too salacious to be sent through the mails, and the passage of the Comstock Act, an 1873 law that was intended to prevent the Postal Service from conveying obscene materials, particularly involving abortion, resulted in the banning of numerous books including the fourteenth century text *The Decameron* by Giovanni Boccaccio, Ernest Hemingway's *For Whom the Bell Tolls*, and even *Lady Chatterley's Lover*, the classic by D.H. Lawrence. Even at present, the Comstock Act has been mentioned as a tool to prevent the dissemination of materials involving in vitro fertilization (IVF) through the mails. The Act was modified by a Supreme Court case in 1957, which restricted postal mailings only to those "without redeeming social importance."

While that decision modified the federal involvement in the mailing of materials, over the past decade attacks against books in the states have increased to the point that over 4,200 books were challenged in states the past year, primarily in school libraries or by school boards and school districts, according to the American Library Association. While the majority of these challenges come from directives or suggestions from just a few organizations, such as "Families for Freedom," they seem to be pursued by very few individuals throughout the nation acting on their own behalf. One woman in Virginia, a devotee of "Families for Freedom," for instance, has pledged to challenge "one schoolbook a week" if they depict what she determines to be "sexual acts." She has challenged dozens of books under Virginia law and has been successful in several instances in getting books removed from school shelves, at least temporarily. To challenge these removals in the courts, or even in administrative hearings is burdensome, time-consuming and expensive.

ACTION IN THE COURTS AND STATES

While litigation involving the Supreme Court and the lower federal courts has been less frequent, there have been occasional cases that have addressed book-banning. While the statutes attacked have generally been enacted by the states, the federal courts have intervened where a denial of due process under the Fourteenth Amendment to the Constitution has been involved. In other words, a state cannot just arbitrarily remove a book from circulation; there must be a judicial or governmental procedure followed to justify such a severe consequence.

In 1982, the seminal Supreme Court case in this regard resulted from an action by a Long Island, New York, school district that directed the removal of several books, including a Pulitzer Prize winner, from the shelves of all middle and high school libraries. They found the books to violate both Christian and Jewish beliefs, to be anti-Semitic and "just filthy." The Supreme Court, in a close decision, held that books could not be removed arbitrarily without proper procedural processes.

Several US Supreme Court Justices have offered opinions on book banning attempts. Justice Louis Brandeis, as long ago as 1928, stated "In frank expression of conflicting opinion lies the greatest promise of wisdom in governmental action; and in suppression lies ordinarily the greatest peril." Justice William O. Douglas, who took a very progressive view, said "Restriction of free thought and free speech is the most dangerous of all perversions," and Justice Potter Steward said "Censorship reflects society's lack of confidence in itself. It is the hallmark of an authoritarian regime."

Thus, the contests are generally in state courts, and the variety of decisions depends on state laws.

In most cases, book banners have failed in their efforts, even in very conservative states with conservative judges. In Oklahoma, for instance, the state supreme court denied efforts to ban certain titles because the law being attacked did not account for differing "community standards" within the state. Several states, most recently Minnesota, have passed laws against book banning unless the banning attempts go through very strict scrutiny, which inevitably defeats the attempts to ban them.

But the attempts to ban books continue and states pass legislation that inevitably ends up being tested in the courts. Utah, in its first statewide ban, outlawed books by the authors Judy Blume and Sarah J. Maas, and several other authors, because they contained what the legislature deemed to be "indecent material." That law has been attacked by "Let Utah Read," a coalition of librarians, teachers, parents and several organizations dedicated to fight banning efforts.

In Alabama and in several other states, much harsher legislation threatens librarians with jailing if they distribute material "harmful to minors," a category that includes "drug-related material, sexual conduct or gender-oriented conduct." In Texas, a school board voted against utilizing textbooks that spoke of climate control or anything critical of the oil and gas industries, and in Florida an arts festival was attacked because some exhibitors displayed children's books with drawings of a "sexual or pornographic" nature. Other state legislatures have offered their own interpretations to legislation designed to "purify" the literature on schools and library shelves.

ORGANIZATIONS, PRO and CON

"Families for Freedom" was started as a grassroots operation during the COVID-19 outbreak when people had far more time to spend in their homes and to scrutinize things such as school curricula and the offerings of local libraries. It quickly grew into a national organization that boasts several hundred branches and well over 100,000 members. Its monthly newsletter, distributed nationally, was edited and offered frequent articles by the late Tish Duvall. Publication has not resumed since her death. Some articles, offered by members of the clergy, had a definite Christian Nationalist tone. There were other similar groups throughout the country that were affiliated with the national organization, with a variety of individual groups or with names of local significance.

On the other side, fighting against banning were organizations such as the American Library Association, The American Booksellers for Free Expression, the American Federation of Teachers, The Authors Guild, PEN America, and numerous publishing and local organizations.

In an interview several months ago, Meredith Bigote of Melbourne Beach, Florida, one of the founders of "Families for Freedom," who said she was involved in many "church and civic organizations," stated that "Families" was begun to eradicate "porn, nudity, and salacious material that endangered children" that was available on school library shelves or used by teachers. Stating that the "United States is basically a Christian nation," she described the organization as "non-partisan, but steeped in conservative Christian values." Ms. Bigote stated that she "is very close to the Catholic church," and in fact, was encouraged in her efforts by her brother, a priest, and one of the authors of newsletter articles. She resigned from the organization she founded several months ago along with another co-founder for "personal reasons." Her brother, who recently left his congregation, was unavailable for comment.

PROFESSIONAL SCRUTINY

Professor Elias Dawson of Stanford University, a nationally recognized psychologist, speaking about efforts to censor or ban books, stated, "We have, unfortunately, seen people overreact in times of crisis or even imagined crises. And a small minority can suddenly be in control of a perceived problem, or even an actual one. Cult-like leaders can lead people astray, people who would normally be unaffected but who are vulnerable and stoked into a dangerous mindset. Think of Jim Jones and those cult followers he led to their deaths.

"In these book-banning cases, people who do not even have children in the schools they attack are often involved, and in many cases, books that are attacked have not even been read by the attackers, who are following the directives of others. A disproportionate number of books under attack are by female authors, Black authors, and contain material that is innocuous. Content available through social media today far exceeds the damage a few words in a well-written book can do.

"A book is a learning experience, and the best policy is to let teachers teach. After all, the biggest challenge today is to get children to read in the first place. It is a sad commentary on our society that librarians, teachers and educators are subject to threats, intimidation and unfortunately, violence for just trying to educate and make this a better society. There is no question that parents have the absolute right to control what their children read, but book banning, questionable at best, should never be based on religious or ideological beliefs in a democratic society. The logical conclusion is that the matter should end there."

THE MOST BANNED TITLES

According to the American Library Association, the titles most attacked are:

To Kill a Mockingbird by Harper Lee

The Catcher in the Rye by J.D. Salinger

Of Mice and Men by John Steinbeck

The Great Gatsby by F. Scott Fitzgerald

1984 by George Orwell

The Adventures of Huckleberry Finn by Mark Twain

The Harry Potter series, by J.K. Rowling

Brave New World by Aldous Huxley

The Color Purple by Alice Walker

The Lord of the Flies by William Golding

CONCLUSION

The language of the First Amendment to the US Constitution would seem to be sufficient to establish the right to author and publish a book without attack. Of course, there are pro-scriptions which are well-established in the law—you can't yell "Fire!" in a crowded theater—but the line beyond that is open to question. You can't defame a person or their reputation, but what is deemed "prurient" by one person is often deemed acceptable by another. We will not resolve these disputes in this article, or even in the courts. At the same time government seems to condone allowing unlimited access to firearms based on an Amendment that is 250 years old. One might think that far more harm can be done by an AK-47 in the hands of an un-stable person than a few words contained in a book.

Or, in the words of a well-known politician, perhaps directed to those who would dictate or direct their moral decisions at his family, "Mind your own damn business."

[Alison Powers contributed to the research and writing of this article]

Mort, Danni, the twins and Katie Springer drove to Travilah for J.J.'s Labor Day barbeque party and festivities, including the marriage of Atticus and Alison. Mort's emails and cell phone overloaded with congratulatory calls and communications immediately after the *Post* article published.

Forty-nine

Labor Day dawned clear, sunny, and hot, a perfect day for the festivities of the day. Chickie hired the same caterers she had used over the past several years since she took over the planning and arrangements, and J.J., to his displeasure, was removed from cheffing duties at the grill to become a full-time host.

Atticus, Alison and their families stayed nearby at the Hilton Garden Inn in Rockville where Chickie had reserved a number of rooms. Included among the guests were Eric Robbins, the *Clarion* publisher, who had flown in with Atticus and Alison. There were the usual local guests, as well as J.J.'s close friend and frequent adversary when he was on the court, retired Justice Anthony Battaglia, now nearing ninety, plus Justice Julius Gallagher, whose life J.J. had saved several years earlier by assessing a critical health emergency and applying CPR.

J.J., who had long been a favorite of court personnel with his down-to-earth and unassuming nature, usually drew a large number of them to these festivities. Supreme Court Police Chief and close friend Travis Anderson was present with his family, as always. So were Alison's parents, brother and sister from New Orleans; Atticus's mother; and, of course, Lupe and her niece Juanita, who babysat the twins when Mort and Danni were at work and who had just graduated from Howard University.

The caterers had set up the seating for about a hundred people, with a center aisle festooned with a red carpet on which the bride would enter. The chairs were outside the kitchen—between it and the barn/garage—and Katie reveled in the opportunity to nose about and seek whatever food she could entice from the crowd.

A bar was set up near the kitchen and white-clad caterers walked among the entourage with hors d'oeuvres as everyone socialized before the wedding ceremony. Lupe and Juanita remained in the kitchen, allegedly supervising the caterers but in actuality awaiting the twins to awaken from their nap.

A string quartet hired by Chickie offered soothing music despite J.J. and Mort's preference for country-western. The music brought the crowd to their feet with a few loud chords to get the wedding services started. J.J. took a position next to a lectern at the front with Katie at his feet wagging her tail and scouring the crowd, looking around for further hand-outs.

"First, I would like to offer greetings to all of you, and say welcome to this event, which has become so much of a pleasant part of our lives," J.J. said. "As usual, Chickie did her impeccable job with the arrangements, but I still relish the old days when I manned the grill. Family, old friends, new friends, all cherished—time marches on. To begin with, and as usual, I have a few announcements." Everyone was silent. For years, they had anticipated J.J. would announce his retirement from the court. Inevitably, he never had.

"I know a lot of you are waiting to hear me say I'm stepping down from the court, but once again, I'm afraid you'll be disappointed. While I've succeeded in making Justice Gallagher reasonable—on occasion—I can't allow the majority to tinker with the Constitution unchecked, so as they say—one more time."

There were a few laughs and applause from the court personnel.

"To tell the truth, though," J.J. continued, "if this wedding thing continues and I get a little more proficient at it, I might just make it a full-time gig." More laughs. "I do take tips." Lots of chuckles.

"Now, as you know, Mort had a great article that published yesterday in the Washington Post, and he's already gotten wonderful feedback. Our bride today, Alison, was a large part of the research for his efforts, and their earlier one, and I'm glad to see that she got the credit she deserves.

"The banning of books is just another attempt by a minority—and I think it's a small minority—to control our thinking by restricting what we read. It is a threat to democracy, and we have had too many threats to democracy in recent years. In case some of those who would restrict our choices of books need advice, let them read the First Amendment and understand that our founders implemented it into the Constitution as a *First* Amendment to emphasize its importance and to avoid exactly what these book banners are trying to accomplish—whether it be in restricting what we can read or even imposing their religious beliefs on us. The tradition of the separation of church and state is sacred, and we need courageous journalists like Mort and Alison to remind us and protect us from those who would attack our freedoms."

Applause.

"However," J.J. continued, "Alison's attributes don't end there. Our loss is to the benefit of the Shelter Rock Clarion, where Alison now serves as editor. Eric Robbins, the publisher and a new friend, is here today, and if you haven't met him yet, make sure you do. A little over a year ago, and because his paper is independent and courageous, and does what newspapers are supposed to do—hold the feet of public officials to the fire when reviewing their professional conduct—Eric's paper was set upon by a bunch of hooligans masquerading as public officials and law enforcement personnel. These small-minded folks swooped in and tried to shut him down, or at least beat him into submission so they could continue to operate without legitimate supervision.

"Thanks to Eric's courage, exacerbated by the loss of his mother because of their illegal conduct, and with his computers and equipment illegally seized, the Clarion never missed a publication date.

"Today, the public officials responsible for those illegal acts have either resigned, gone into hiding, or in two cases I'm aware of, are being prosecuted. And rightly so. We are happy to have Eric with us, and we know, with Alison on board, that his paper will continue its fearless pursuit of truth and honesty. There is no greater need in our nation than for a free and fearless press. I should add that Eric has reached a settlement with the insurance company representing Shelter Rock because of the lawless conduct of its officials, and that he has arranged to buy Fielder's Foods, the largest grocery establishment in Shelter Rock, and will rename it Margery's Market in honor of his late mother. The present owner will not need it because of his incarceration."

Louder applause.

"In addition, Eric is taking the balance of the funds from that settlement and establishing a scholarship in his mother's honor at the Kansas University School of Journalism and Mass Communications."

More applause.

"Finally, speaking of Alison, who will be walking down this aisle in a few minutes, I can report that she is now taking flying lessons—I wonder why—and that momentum is building in Shelter Rock for Atticus to run for mayor in the upcoming elections. He will not, of course, be endorsed by the Clarion because of a conflict of interest, but we wish him well. Another surprise, which even my daughter Danni doesn't know, is that Lupe's niece Juanita, who has also become one of our family, has just been accepted as a student at the American University Law School. She did it on her own, because she didn't want folks to think that Danni's influence helped her to get in. And now, if the wedding party will take its positions up here with me, we'll get this show on the road."

Wild applause. Danni looked around, not seeing Juanita, and leaned over to Mort and said, "Where is she? I don't see either her or Lupe."

"Getting the twins ready for their big moment," Mort said, as he got up and led Danni to the front of the gathering, where they stood on both sides of J.J. as Matron of Honor and Best Man. The orchestra struck up the Bridal Chorus from Lohengrin by Richard Wagner, "Here Comes the Bride." On cue, Alison appeared on the arm of her father and walked to the lectern.

In the back of the gathering, Lupe and Juanita held the twins, Dakota and Meggy, dressed in matching short outfits, and set them down by the red runner. Lupe put a small box in Dakota's hands and directed him to walk down the aisle with his sister. The twins toddled forward, Dakota clutching the ring box in his tiny hand. As they reached the lectern, Dakota reached up to hand the ring to Mort, looked at him, and said, "Papi."

Mort jerked his head toward Lupe, and said, "My God, he's speaking Spanish."

From her spot in the back, with a broad smile, Lupe said, "Sí, he smart like his Mama."

Acknowledgments

The expression "it takes a village" was never more appropriate than when applied to a novel. Without such patient collaborators, this book would never have seen the light of day. It required an extraordinary amount of research and travel, and the willingness of many individuals to give of their time and expertise as acknowledged below:

- Sharon and Bill Raker are more than first readers and critics, and Bill, the brother I never had, gave far more than one could expect in many respects.

- The folks at Calumet Editions. Josh Weber, Ian Leask, and particularly Gary Lindberg, were always there, labored long hours, and put up with all my eccentricities and shortcomings. Copyeditor Rick Polad did an incredible job as he pored over the manuscript time and again and was always right on point.

- I would be remiss if I failed to mention Avi Meshar, webmaster, friend, and fortunately a great technician, who bailed me out more times than one should admit, and whose expertise saved this manuscript time and again.

- Dr. Irwin Hirsch, professor and clinical psychologist, has made more contributions than I care to admit.

About the Author

Alan Miller began his love of journalism early in life, and it carried through to serving as editor of his high school newspaper, writing the senior variety show, and becoming sports editor of the local village newspaper at fifteen, which led to a sports reporter position at *Newsday* at sixteen. Since then, he majored in journalism and political science in college, became an attorney, worked on several other newspapers, and taught in colleges, universities, and law schools as well as for the National Institute for Trial Advocacy. As a weekly columnist for a Long Island, New York, newspaper, he won a first-place designation from the New York Press Association, as well as a best column in Bowling magazine, wrote for the late Joe Franklin's magazine, and began appearing on television on Franklin's nationally televised program as a guest. For the last quarter century, he has been the host-producer of an award-winning local access TV program, "Access to Democracy," now networked in thirty-five Minnesota cities and recently created a new local access TV program in Minnesota entitled Writers Corner. He resides in Minnesota with his wife Sharon and a springer spaniel rescue named Katie.